Shirley Holmquist
& Aunt Wilma
The Most Celebrated SCANDINAVIAN DETECTIVES Who Ever Lived!
WHODUNIT?
Janet Letnes Martin

ALSO BY JANET LETNESS MARTIN

Reiste Til Amerika
Cream and Bread
Second Helpings of Cream and Bread

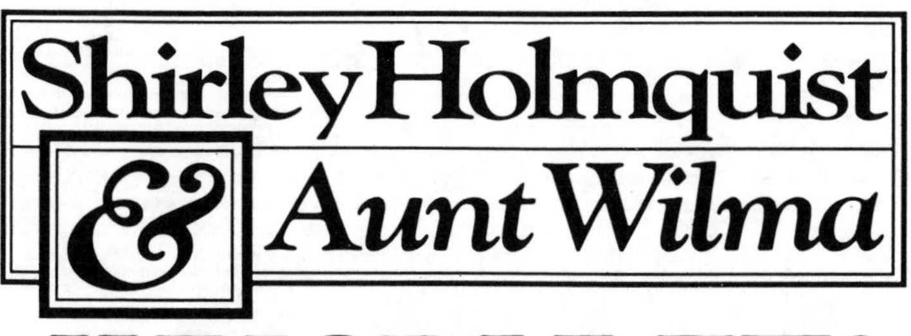

WHODUNIT?

By JANET LETNES MARTIN

MARTIN HOUSE PUBLICATIONS
Hastings, Minnesota 55033

Printed in the United States of America
Published by Martin House Publications
Box 274, Hastings, Minnesota 55033

Library of Congress Catalog Card Number 88-60775
ISBN 0-9613437-2-9

FIRST EDITION
Illustrated by Michael Yahn
Edited by Eunice Wold Pearson
Photos by McGoon Studios, Hastings, Minnesota
Cover design by Koechel/Peterson Design, Inc., Minneapolis

To Shirley & Aunt Wilma

ACKNOWLEDGMENTS

Mange tusen tak and greatful acknowledgments to Eunice Wold Pearson, my editor; Michael Yahn, my illustrator; Shirley and Aunt Wilma, my friends; and above all to Neil and our girls for putting up with my kitchen table writing.

CONTENTS

INTRODUCTION

London had Sherlock Holmes and Dr. Watson, but if Sir Arthur Conan Doyle's detectives could somehow be transported to Heartsburg, U.S.A., the land of lutefisk, lefse, and patriotic, hard-working, sensible Lutherans, they couldn't hold a candle to Shirley Holmquist and her Aunt Wilma Watson. Though some might call them nosey

Shirley Holmquist and Aunt Wilma Watson

Scandinavian busybodies, Shirley and Aunt Wilma are certain that the problems and irritations they've brought to light have gained Heartsberg the proud status of All-American City. Even Sheriff Roy Larson, who has never dealt in murders, drug busts, and big-time robberies, has grudgingly admitted that their good coffee and common sense have helped him out of a particularly sticky jam.

Once Ole Axelson jokingly told Hardware Man Benson that Shirley and Aunt Wilma must be shirttail relatives of the famed London pair, but upon close examination, successful mystery solving is the only thing that Holmquist/Watson and Holmes/Watson have in common:

SHIRLEY HOLMQUIST
Lives in white frame house in Heartsberg.
Baptized and Confirmed a Lutheran.
Attended country school to eighth grade.
Married Ed Holmquist, a Swede.
Has one married daughter, Gloria Jean.
Early to bed, early to rise.
Drinks strong egg coffee.
Tidy housekeeper.
Never tried smoking.
Assists local sheriff.
Played the piano for Sunday School opening exercises.
Used common sense in solving mysteries.
Favorite expression: "It's right under our noses, Aunt Wilma!"

AUNT WILMA WATSON
Single.
Cared for parents until they died.
Traveled three times — to Winnipeg, Duluth, and Yellowstone Park.
Member, Women's Christian Temperance Union.
Never cast a ballot.
Played croquet in younger years at church picnics.

SHERLOCK HOLMES
Lived in London apartment.
No church affiliation.
Studied at Oxford and Cambridge.
Never married.
No children.
Night owl.
Drank hard liquor.
Messy as could be.
Smoked incessantly.
Assisted Scotland Yard.
Played the violin.
Used scientific method in solving mysteries.
Favorite expression: "Elementary, my dear Watson."

DR. WATSON
Married three times.
Cared for patients until they died.
Traveled three continents.
Drank all sorts of spirits.
Member of Parliament.
Played cricket at the club.

CHAPTER 1

THE CASE OF

The Character Lines in Chenille

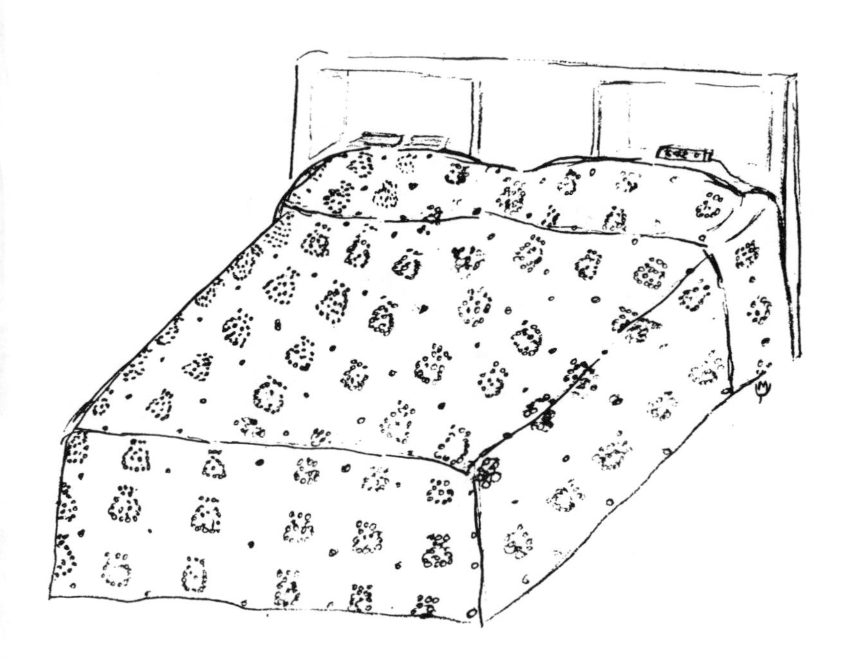

The Character Lines in Chenille

Ed was resting in his easy chair after a long day at the post office. "The way the government operates," he complained, "I shouldn't have been surprised that they brought in a divorced outsider to help with the Christmas mail rush. Velda Wagner has no idea that Ole Axelson likes his mail delivered to the meat market, even though his home address is on the envelope. She doesn't know that Anton Anderson on RR3 is in the nursing home, and that Anton Anderson on RR2 spends his winters in Florida and wants his mail forwarded."

Shirley agreed. "It is hard to get decent help nowadays. But, Ed, you only have two weeks left, and then you'll be done working for good. It is retirement that should concern you now. You need a hobby, or you'll end up having a heart attack. And what would I do if you died? And even if you didn't die, you'd better know I'm too busy to care for an invalid."

Lately, retirement had begun to weigh heavily on Ed's mind. He had given forty-five good years to the United States Postal Service, and soon he'd be finished, for good. It was a scary thought, because even though Shirley said he'd have time to do whatever he wanted, he had no idea what that was. It would be enough of an adjustment to be at home with her day in and day out. But he guessed he had better come to grips with retirement, because as Shirley had often reminded him, "Hans Rasmussen didn't, and he died."

Ed didn't want to think about it anymore. He put on his coat and hat.

"Where are you going at this time of night?" asked Shirley.

Ed sighed. "I'm just going out to check on the weather."

Shirley should have been a man, he thought. She would have been a natural in the F.B.I. or C.I.A. He was a private person, and he couldn't understand how she seemed to thrive on keeping track of everyone and their footprints. And one day, if she stuck out her nose too far, he'd be thrust into the limelight too. Just the thought of it made the sweat stand out on his forehead. He decided to walk around the block.

When he returned, Shirley met him at the door. "Where in the world have you been? Gloria Jean just called long distance from the Cities, and she didn't even get a chance to say hello to you."

"Well," said Ed, "you usually talk for both of us anyway. What did she want?"

"We've got a big problem," said Shirley. "She and Merle haven't received our box of Christmas gifts yet. I mailed it over two weeks ago. You'd better run a trace on it first thing in the morning."

"Did she say anything else?"

"I told her it wasn't my idea to mail the gifts. It seemed senseless since postage is so high, and they are planning to come home for Christmas anyway. You were the one who insisted it be done in case a storm blew up and they couldn't travel."

"Did you tell her not to start out if the weather looked bad?"

"She wanted to know what we wanted for Christmas, and I told her we didn't need anything. I didn't mention that you could use a new cardigan, and that I'm about due for a new nightgown. If I had to go to the hospital with the one I have, I'd feel like crawling into a hole. But I suppose I'll get a blouse I can't wear with anything, and you'll get another flannel shirt."

Ed decided to go to bed. Shirley wasn't answering his questions anyway. Besides, he was tired of hearing about lost packages, tired of sorting through Christmas cards, tired of listening to Shirley, and just plain tired.

The next morning Shirley called Aunt Wilma to tell her about the lost Christmas box.

"I always send as little as possible," said Aunt Wilma. "About ten years ago, I sent a birthday card with a dollar in it to my cousin Ethel in northern Minnesota. I don't know if the Indians took it or what, but I know she never received it, because she never thanked me for it."

"Well, this was more than $1.00," said Shirley. "I went a little overboard this year and bought Gloria Jean and Merle a beautiful white chenille bedspread in the Americana Pineapple pattern. I just hope Merle has enough sense to keep his boots off the bed. He works shifts, and sometimes just before he leaves, he takes a nap with them on. I don't know why Gloria Jean doesn't put her foot down, but I guess it's not for me to say. I sent their daughter, Mary

Jane, a hat and some mittens. She has so many toys, it's a sin. Now I suppose they're lost too."

Shirley hung up the phone and went to the post office to mail a letter she had written to Gloria Jean earlier that morning. She could have sent it with Ed, but she wanted to get another look at Velda Wagner.

Twice before, Shirley had seen her, once at the post office and once at the drug store. Velda had rented a room above Benson's Hardware for the four weeks she would be in town.

Shirley mailed the letter, got a good look at Velda, and returned home. She was glad Ed had been in the back room so he couldn't see her. She knew he didn't like her coming to the post office because he never knew what she'd say to him or anyone else.

That night Ed told her, "I put a trace on the box, but nothing has turned up. That's the first time I've lost anything."

"Someone must have taken it," said Shirley.

Ed was tired and bit back. "Who are you planning to accuse?"

"I'm not accusing anyone yet," said Shirley, "but a package just doesn't disappear into thin air. My hunch is that you don't have to look any further than home plate to find the thief.

"I think it's Velda who stole it," she continued. "When I walked by her car today, I saw a couple of throw pillows in the backseat. She had removed the 'Under Penalty of Law' tags, so if she doesn't have more respect for the law than that, she might well have taken the bedspread. And when I was at the post office today . . ."

"For what?" broke in Ed.

"Oh, just to mail a letter I forgot to give you. Anyway, I watched Velda, and there wasn't one customer she looked straight in the eye. Now what does that say?"

"Not much," said Ed.

"Well, do you remember the day you took the box to the post office?" continued Shirley. "Velda would have had plenty of time to take it when you came home at noon. I paid $35.00 for that bedspread, and I'm going to find it if it's the last thing I do."

Ed knew that was true as surely as he knew his name. "Well, how do you propose to find out if she took it?"

"Here's my plan," said Shirley. "Tomorrow afternoon at 2:00, tell Velda she can go home and rest, and that you'll call her when you need her back. Phone her at 4:30, and tell her to report to work immediately. And I'll be there waiting."

"Waiting for what?" asked Ed.

"Never mind. Just do as I say."

Ed agreed, because no matter how crazy the plan sounded, Shirley would hound him until she got her way.

The next afternoon, Shirley was waiting at the post office as Velda walked in, looking as though she had just gotten up from bed.

"Come here, Ed," whispered Shirley. "It was Velda all right. The evidence is all over her face."

"What evidence?" asked Ed.

"Chenille bedspread marks!" Shirley nearly shouted the words.

Ed shook his head. He hadn't noticed the marks, but then who, but Shirley, would have?

"Well, I guess I'll have to call the 'higher-ups' and get them here to investigate," he said. "You were right, Shirley. No one can get decent help nowadays. It makes a guy wonder if he should retire."

CHAPTER 2

THE CASE OF

The Missing Merger Pamphlets

The Missing Merger Pamphlets

Aunt Wilma was in a stew. She had spent all Thursday afternoon folding and stapling the pamphlet *If God Had Wanted Us to Merge, He Wouldn't Have Created So Many Denominations to Begin With,* that were to be passed out at the annual meeting on Sunday night. On Saturday when she came to fulfill her Altar Guild duties, she discovered they had been taken from the table in the back of the church where she had carefully stacked them. After alerting the pastor, Aunt Wilma rang up Shirley.

She hated to talk to Shirley about this merger matter. It had been a sore spot between them since '62 when she and thirty-four others who wanted nothing to do with a merged Lutheran church, decided to leave First Lutheran of the Good Shepherd, and Shirley and Ed had refused to join them. Their daughter, Gloria Jean, had just been elected Secretary-Treasurer of the Luther League, and she had convinced them that she couldn't in good conscience back out of her commitment. It pained Aunt Wilma that Shirley and Ed had ignored the admonition to "train up a child in the way he should go . . ." and instead bowed to the whim of their daughter, but nothing she had said had changed their minds.

Despite that sore spot, Aunt Wilma knew she could

count on Shirley to help solve the pamphlet theft, because when there was a mystery involved, Shirley would have even helped the Methodists. That was the kind of person she was.

Still upset, Aunt Wilma gave Shirley the details. She had placed the pamphlets on the table late Thursday afternoon. The only ones in the church on Friday were the pastor and young Mrs. Ole Anderson who had come in about 2:30 p.m. to type the bulletin. That evening the Mary Circle had invited the Martha Circle to their annual beef-n-bean potluck (barbecues, beans, coleslaw, cake, and coffee), and she and Mrs. Tina Gunderson, a recent widow who lived behind the church, who was also a member of the Tuesday morning Martha Circle, went together.

"I left the church about 7:30 that evening and went straight home," said Wilma. "I didn't see anyone else leave except Mrs. Gunderson who was cradling a bunch of dirty dishtowels she was taking home to wash. And I'm not sure what time the Mary Circle serving committee left because they went out the back door which I couldn't see." (Aunt Wilma could relate these details about the comings and goings at the church because she had recently moved into the new Sunny-Side Acres With a View apartment complex, located directly across the street from Hope for the Living Word Lutheran and overlooked a field of clover.

She continued, "This morning the pastor came at 8:30 and the four confirmands came rushing in for class just before 9:00. They left at 11:00 and the pastor at 11:20. It's now 12:30, and the pamphlets are gone. It's just a shame, but the thief must be either young Mrs. Ole Anderson or one of the confirmands, don't you think, Shirley? But what reason under the sun would there be for young Mrs. Ole Anderson to steal them? And even if we looked the confirmands straight in the eyes and questioned them, it probably wouldn't do any good because kids nowadays don't look guilty like they did in my day."

"Aunt Wilma, how about if I attend church with you tomorrow?" Shirley offered.

Just as she promised, Shirley picked up Aunt Wilma for the 11:00 service, and as they stepped inside, Shirley felt as though she had gone back in time. Hope for the Living Word Lutheran Church was just like the one she had attended as a child. There were black hymnals in the pew racks, a big, black furnace grate on the floor providing heat for the entire sanctuary, and a persnickety, tired-looking woman pumping *"Faith of our Fathers"* on the organ.

Aunt Wilma led the way into the eighth pew. It was probably the one she sat in all the time, thought Shirley.

She craned her neck to see the four confirmands sitting in the front row. From the back, none of them appeared fidgety or nervous. Across the aisle she spotted young Mrs. Ole Anderson with a disgusted look on her face. But she had an unruly little one sitting next to her whom she was trying to keep in line. Mrs. Tina Gunderson sat down next to Shirley. One of her knees looked swollen, and the heel of her right shoe was awfully scuffed up. Poor thing must have slipped on the ice, Shirley thought.

During the sermon Shirley's mind wandered to the details Aunt Wilma had related. And then, out of the blue, the answer came!

After she shook the pastor's hand at the close of the service, Shirley went to look at the wooden table in the back of the church. There was the evidence she needed — a big, milky-white stain.

Shirley hated to tell Aunt Wilma what she knew, but she really had no choice. As the two drank coffee in Aunt Wilma's apartment, Shirley said, "I don't know why she did it, maybe only the good Lord knows, but it was Mrs. Gunderson who stole the pamphlets."

Before Aunt Wilma could respond, Shirley went on. "It was a simple matter of putting two and two together. When you said that she left the Friday night potluck with a bundle of dirty dishtowels, I wondered why she was taking them home since her Circle wasn't hostessing. And isn't it strange that she left by the front door when the back door would have meant a shorter walk to her house and no ice on the sidewalk to contend with?"

"I'm sure Mrs. Gunderson offered to take the dishtowels so she would have something in which to conceal the pamphlets she was bound and determined to take. She must have tiptoed upstairs into the dark sanctuary, spread the wet dishtowels on the table, slipped the pamphlets inside, and in her haste to leave, caught her heel in the furnace grate, and twisted her knee trying to free herself."

Aunt Wilma couldn't argue with Shirley. She remembered how the late Gunnar Gunderson, the leader of the anti-merger forces, had grabbed people by their collars and tried to force them to believe as he did. And maybe his own wife didn't. Maybe she was one of the thirty-five only because she was a dutiful helpmate.

"Well, Shirley," she said, "We can at least be as big as the Lord and forgive and forget. On Judgment Day we'll find out which Lutherans are in the Lamb's Book of Life."

CHAPTER 3

THE CASE OF

The Ribbon Snatchers

The Ribbon Snatchers

Shirley was busy cleaning out the storeroom. Her Circle was going to pack clothes for the annual spring African mission drive, and she was sorting through some of Gloria Jean's old things to see what she could give away. It was getting to be that time of year, anyway, to go through boxes and closets and air things out. She really didn't know if it made any sense to send clothes to the heathens. She had heard that the Communists stole the boxes right off the boats, and that's why in pictures they were either half-naked or wrapped up in some gaudy strips of cloth that didn't look very Christian.

But, she had to give these clothes away. They were collecting dust, and Gloria Jean's daughter, Mary Jane, had remarked she wouldn't be caught dead wearing them. Had she lived through the Depression, Shirley figured she wouldn't be so picky. But Gloria Jean had spoiled her, and there was nothing to do about that now.

She pulled out four pairs of spiked heels, even the tips in perfectly good condition. How sad, she thought, that kids today discard shoes without regard for the money they cost. When she was young she had worn out many a sole walking four miles to school each day, and she had been thankful for any kind of shoe she got. Oh, well, she decided, these might as well go to Africa. Seeing pictures of barefoot kids bothered her a lot.

A box marked "Gloria Jean's Skirts and Dresses, '59, '60, '61" was next. And on top lay her daughter's first big 4-H sewing project, an aqua gingham-checked gathered skirt. The two rows of rick-rack at the bottom were now yellowed, but they were straight! She had insisted that Gloria Jean rip them off three times until they were sewn perfectly. And it paid off, Shirley thought fondly, as she remembered the blue ribbon Gloria Jean had received. She folded the skirt and set it aside. Maybe she could give it away some other time, but not now. There were just too many good memories connected with it.

But the purple and white flowered spaghetti strap dress with its matching lavender bolero jacket, was another story. As she unfolded it, the old anger came back. This dress, which should have been State Fair bound, had been beaten out by an outfit worn by Betty Kaye Bloom, a first year member of their Don't We Seam Nice 4-H Club. And the whole episode, once again, flashed into Shirley's mind.

Gloria Jean had been in the tenth grade when Betty Kaye and her mother Bunny moved to town. Bunny, an independent, floozy-looking divorcee had gotten a job at the bank and rented the upstairs of Mrs. Florence Ellingson's home.

Mrs. Ellingson, a kind old widow who sewed together quilt pieces for missions all winter and tended her flower gardens all summer, took in strays. Besides the Blooms, she housed nine cats who had at various times showed up at her door and stayed. Her house was a mess — cats curled in chairs all over, quilt pieces piled miles high on her Singer, and plant slips of every imaginable kind growing in plastic cups on every dusty window sill. But she had a good heart and would give the shirt off her back to anyone, whether it was needed or not.

The Blooms hadn't been in town for more than a month when Mrs. Ellingson convinced Betty Kaye to join 4-H. She reasoned that if someone didn't teach Betty Kaye how to cook and sew, she'd end up just like her mother.

While Mrs. Ellingson's intentions had been good, after the first meeting that Betty Kaye and her mother attended, Shirley smelled trouble. Instead of hemming dishtowels and making a felt scissor case as all beginners did, Bunny insisted that Betty Kaye sew a leisure-time outfit that would be her Fair project. She assured everyone that her sister, a sewing machine demonstrator and alterations lady for Montgomery Ward in Des Moines, had taught Betty Kaye all the basics. And since the Blooms acted like pushy, insistent city slickers, no one felt comfortable questioning them.

Shirley hadn't wanted to doubt Betty Kaye's ability, but she was as certain as she could be that without a lick of guidance from her mother, Betty Kaye would never have the stick-to-it-iveness to complete the project.

And when she and Aunt Wilma headed up the walk to Mrs. Ellingson's home for Garden Club the week before Fair time, Shirley knew her assessment was right on target. There in a lawn chair, wearing bright red shorts and a red polka dot halter top pinned at the shoulders, sat Bunny, filing her nails. Betty Kaye, half asleep, reclined on a blanket, listening to her transistor radio.

"Fyda," Shirley whispered to Aunt Wilma as they walked to the door. "Instead of lying outside half naked, those grown women should be helping Mrs. Ellingson get ready for Garden Club or be sewing Betty Kaye's 4-H project."

She averted her eyes as Aunt Wilma nodded in her direction and said, "It is getting to be a hot one today."

Once inside, they couldn't believe their eyes! Evidently Mrs. Ellingson had done some deep, serious housecleaning. Oh, there was still junk lying around and cats curled all over, but Aunt Wilma noticed that the curtains had been washed, starched, and stretched. Shirley couldn't detect a trace of the black skid marks that for six years had been etched into the linoleum floor by the late Mr. Ellingson's boots. The front room had even been dusted. Shirley remembered that *The Lutheran Stockholm Connection in the Midwest* had been next to *Cats and How They Curl* on the bottom shelf of the bookcase. Now they were on the second shelf, with the bottom one taken up by a big ceramic cat.

Shirley and Aunt Wilma didn't linger after lunch. With Fair week just around the corner, Shirley wanted to get home to supervise the final touches on Gloria Jean's project.

Actually, she and Gloria Jean were getting on each other's nerves. Gloria Jean didn't want any more advice, and Shirley pleaded for her to listen, because if she had told her once, she had told her a hundred times, it was the little things, the finishing touches that made the difference between a blue and purple ribbon.

But all the advice in the world didn't matter. When the clothes had been judged and the grand champion ribbon awarded to Betty Kaye Bloom for her continental blue and red striped coordinating skirt, shorts, and blouse, Shirley was numb. Her stomach knotted up in the same way it did when the pastor had announced that the majority in the church had voted to get the new red hymnals.

Shirley examined Betty Kaye's outfit closely. It had been sewn so perfectly, it could have been store bought. But the judges' decision had been made. There was nothing she could do about it. It was the red hymnal vote all over again.

At the Style Revue the next evening, the 4-H'ers modeled their outfits. As Gloria Jean got in line, Shirley whispered, "Hold your head high, dear. This is unfair, but the Scripture says the sun shines on the unjust as well as the just."

But things only got worse! It wasn't just Betty Kaye, but also her mother wearing an identical leisure-time outfit, who waltzed onto the stage. Shirley felt she would explode as she watched them prance and strut like ponies in a three-ring circus, Betty Kaye with her phony ear-to-ear grin and Bunny's spider-veined, skinny legs sticking out from underneath the blue and red striped shorts.

Shirley, Gloria Jean, and Aunt Wilma sat in silence on the ride home. As they pulled up to the curb, Aunt Wilma said, "Why don't you come in for some angel food cake? I have something I want to show you."

While the coffee was perking, Aunt Wilma opened

her Montgomery Ward catalog to the dry goods section. There, in color, on page 425 was the material the Blooms had used. "That proves it," said Aunt Wilma. "Bunny's sister, the sewing machine and alterations lady, sewed their outfits."

"I suspected that all along," muttered Gloria Jean.

"I'm not so sure," broke in Shirley. "Oh, they might have gotten the material from Bunny's sister at the reduced employee's rate, but when I examined Betty Kaye's outfit, I knew it had been stitched on a Singer, not a Montgomery Ward machine. Believe me, I can recognize a Singer stitch a mile away. And because the two outfits fit so perfectly, they had to have been sewn by someone who could fit them every step of the way, and that would be impossible for someone living in Des Moines.

"I knew Betty Kaye didn't sew it because there were no needle marks on the darts. She's had no sewing experience, so she'd have had to pin and baste them. And it was easy to eliminate Bunny. She works in the bank all day and is over forty, so she wouldn't have been able to see well enough to sew at night. Besides, when we went to the Ellingson home for Garden Club, her halter top was pinned. If she couldn't even mend, I knew she certainly couldn't sew.

"So that brought me down to Mrs. Ellingson. She not only has a Singer machine, but she sews beautifully. And the kind soul probably couldn't say no to Betty Kaye when she asked for help. The way I have it figured, Betty Kaye and Bunny did Mrs. Ellingson's spring housecleaning in exchange for the sewing. After all the times we've been in her home for Garden Club, it seems unlikely that she would suddenly change her cleaning habits and scrub things that she hadn't touched in years."

"And the dear lady probably never dreamed that her fine sewing would cause such damage and heartache," mused Aunt Wilma.

Shirley folded the purple and white dress and put it into the mission box. It had too many bittersweet memories to hold onto any longer. Maybe some little girl in Africa would think it a grand champion!

CHAPTER 4

THE CASE OF

The Burgled Bulb

The Burgled Bulb

Shirley couldn't sleep for love nor money. It was two hours past midnight, and she was as wide awake as if it had been 5:45 a.m., the time she usually started her day. There was no reason under the sun, she told herself for the tenth time that night, why only twelve of the thirteen iris bulbs the Garden Club had planted around the World War II Memorial in the city park, had come up. And, as she told Ed before they went to sleep, the Garden Club had paid good money for those bulbs, they looked healthy when they were planted, and the winter hadn't been as rough as predicted, so someone, for whatever reason, must have dug up a bulb and stolen it.

Ed, as usual, was no help. "You're making a mountain out of a molehill," he said. "No one in his right mind would steal one of the bulbs. And it's certainly not something to lose sleep over."

Shirley got up. There was no sense lying in bed wasting time. Anyway, Ed's snoring was getting on her nerves. Might as well make myself useful, she thought, as she began to shell the pecans Ed's brother had brought back for them from his winter stay down South.

She hated to have a light on at this time of night. Between Signe Svendahl, her back-door neighbor who was letting her cat in and out every two hours, and Harold Odegaard, the old man across the street who was up going to the bathroom all night, the neighborhood was lit up like Las Vegas. And one, if not both, would ask Ed the next morning what was wrong because they had seen the Holmquist's light on. It was one of those things she didn't like about living in town. There was just no privacy, and some people were too nosey for their own good.

The shelling done, Shirley put the pecans in the freezer to save for Christmas baking and went back to bed. It felt good to have accomplished something, and hearing Ed's snores made her feel even better that she had done it without his help. Even though he always volunteered, he made such a mess that she spent more time cleaning up after him than it was worth. "Now, if I could only figure out who took the iris bulb," she murmured as she drifted off to sleep.

Morning came too soon, and Shirley found herself nodding off during the sermon. She was thankful she'd have a chance to go home and nap before she picked up Aunt Wilma for a Sunday afternoon ride and early supper at their house.

The two drove straight to the World War II Memorial to see if they could detect anything unusual. And, sure enough, there was evidence! The ground had not only sunk where the missing bulb had been planted, but it was obvious to Shirley that the bulb had been dug out by a hand spade.

It couldn't have been, as Aunt Wilma suggested, the work of a dog, because in March, just before the Garden Club members raked off the leaves they had put on as a winter covering during Mulch and Munch Days, the ground had been neatly covered, just as they had left it.

"And, Aunt Wilma," said Shirley, "a dog wouldn't know enough to cover up the area after it dug out the bulb. Someone deliberately stealing, though, would do just that."

When they returned to the Holmquist's for supper, Shirley was so bothered that she nearly caught her hand in the mixer as she whipped the cream for the J-ello.

"It's not so much the bulb," said Aunt Wilma, "but the principle of the whole thing that gets me."

"Well," Shirley sighed, "it's the bulb too. It's going to mess up everything for us. You remember we planted those thirteen bulbs as a living tribute to the thirteen charter members of the Garden Club. And even if one of our charters, Mrs. Olaf Carlson, God rest her soul, has passed on, you can bet your boots she told Amanda about the living tribute, and that woman who never found much time to visit her mother when she was alive, will be here with bells on, taking the glory and counting the bulbs to make sure one is planted in her mother's honor."

"Well," said Aunt Wilma, "you can tell her it was my bulb that didn't come up."

"That's not the point," said Shirley, agitation rising in her voice. "We told the VFW Auxiliary, and they told the newspaper that we had bought and planted thirteen bulbs as a tribute, not only to our charter members, but to all who had died in the service of our country. At the Memorial Day service which marks the 44th anniversary of the Battle of Normandy, we're going to be thanked publicly for beautifying the park with thirteen Normandy

Invasion Memorial Irises."

Shirley took Aunt Wilma home earlier than usual because she was all pooped out from not getting enough sleep the previous night. Besides, she wanted to do some thinking and backtracking on her own without any distractions.

She pulled her secretary's notebook from the dresser drawer. Maybe by reviewing the minutes of last year's Garden Club meetings, she'd be able to solve the mystery of the missing iris bulb or at least have some idea who the culprit was.

Climbing into her flannel nightie and putting on her nighttime glasses, she began to read:

August 8th

The August meeting of the Garden Club was called to order by Mrs. Sven Vegdahl at the home of Mrs. Julian Opdahl. We opened with the Pledge of Allegiance to the flag, followed by the Gardener's Prayer. Roll call was taken. Mrs. Lars Anders and Mrs. Sam Oldenhaug were absent. The secretary's report was given by Mrs. Ed Holmquist. It was approved as read. Mrs. Johnny Ellingson gave the treasurer's report. The club has a grand total of $1,874.53 on hand. Mrs. Julian Opdahl presented a bill for $3.19 for a box of get-well cards and a few stamps. Mrs. Johnny Ellingson made a motion to pay the bill. It was seconded by Mrs. Ed Holmquist. Mrs. Julian Opdahl said she sent a get well card to Mrs. Lars Anders and had heard she was getting along better with her hip. There was no old business.

Mrs. Ben Soderberg read a letter from the VFW Auxiliary asking for a donation of $25.00 from the Garden Club to help defray the cost of the rose bushes that had been planted earlier in the summer. Discussion followed. Mrs. Julian Opdahl said she thought the rose bushes were a waste of money since the Farmer's Almanac had predicted a winter like '36, and that would certainly kill them for sure. Mrs. Otto Dahlberg said she felt she was speaking for most of the group in thinking the city should right well have donated some money for the rose bushes since property taxes had gone up so terrifically, and the city had gone hog wild in buying Christmas decorations last year, and should have had enough sense to put some funds away for rainy day projects like this, especially since it was planned so far in advance. Everyone agreed. Mrs. Wilma Watson said she thought the VFW could pay for their own rose bushes with their bingo royalties since she had heard there was an awful lot of gambling going on. Mrs. Johnny Ellingson also felt that $25.00 was an awful lot of money for the VFW to beg, but maybe the Garden Club could compromise and save face by offering to buy and plant some iris bulbs. She had just read in Gurney's about a new variety of irises that were not only zone 1-5 winter hardy, but were also called the Normandy Invasion Memorial Irises. With a name like that, they would be just the ticket to plant since the Memorial Day service was going to be a remembrance of the Normany Invasion. She suggested the club plant thirteen bulbs in honor of the thirteen charter members, and that they order them from Gurney's since the company was real good to send a baker's dozen for the price of twelve, which was $5.14. Mrs. Lawrence Hilberg said she thought Mrs. Johnny Ellingson had a good idea, but maybe they should buy eighteen irises and plant one in honor of all the members of the Garden Club, not just the charters. Mrs. Thor Oldenhaug said she really didn't think it necessary to buy another 1/2 dozen bulbs because all the new members, except for her sister-in-law, Mrs. Sam Oldenhaug, who was at home with a toothache, never showed up for meetings or work days anyway. And she knew it wouldn't make any difference to her sister-in-law if she had a bulb planted in her honor since she always went to the Memorial Day service in Hivdahl to visit her husband's grave. Mrs. Thor Oldenhaug made a motion they allow Mrs. Johnny Ellingson to buy thirteen iris bulbs. Mrs. Johnny Ellingson seconded it and told everyone to come and plant the bulbs the last Saturday of August, provided she got the okay from the VFW Auxiliary. Motion passed. Mrs. Wilma Watson suggested the club buy $500.00 worth of savings bonds since the checking account was getting big. Mrs. Ed Holmquist seconded the suggestion. Motion passed. Mrs. Sven Vegdahl reminded everyone of the upcoming Labor Day bus tour to see the mums and fall flowers at the North Dakota International Peace Gardens. The business meeting was adjourned. Mrs. Anton Iverson read a reading entitled, *When the Frost has Taken the Last Bloom of Summer, Don't Wither with It.* She also gave a demonstration on making pink carnations out of Kleenex, gave a tissue carnation to each member, and told them that before they knew it, Spring would be around the corner. Mrs. Julian Opdahl served some delicious bars.

Respectfully submitted,
Mrs. Ed Holmquist

Nothing there, thought Shirley, and she continued to read.

September 12th

The September meeting was called to order by President Mrs. Sven Vegdahl at the home of Mrs. Anton Iverson. We opened with the Pledge of Allegiance to the flag and the Gardener's Prayer. Roll call was taken, and all were present. Mrs. Sven Vegdahl thanked all the regulars for coming to plant the iris bulbs. Mrs. Julian Opdahl read a thank-you note sent to the Garden Club from Mrs. Lars Anders. She said her hip was coming along well. Mrs. Ed Holmquist gave the secretary's report. It was approved as read. Mrs. Johnny Ellingson gave the treasurer's report and said she had bought $500.00 worth of U.S. savings bonds as instructed. Mrs. Sven Vegdahl commented on what a fun trip the Peace Garden tour had been and told Mrs. Sam Oldenhaug it was too bad she hadn't been able to attend . . ."

"Why, it's right in front of my nose," Shirley exclaimed. "Will Aunt Wilma ever be surprised!"

But Aunt Wilma had also done some of her own investigating, and she stopped by the Holmquist's after her morning walk.

"Shirley," she said excitedly, "Mrs. Johnny Ellingson has two Normandy Invasion Memorial Irises growing beside the gate of her white picket fence."

Shirley smiled. "Aunt Wilma, I suspected her too since everyone knows she has no guilt feelings about snapping an African Violet leaf from a plant in a bank or someone's home. But it was her idea to plant the thirteen bulbs. I think she has them because she talked Gurney's out of giving her a couple more free ones. That's just the way she operates. Now, I'll bet if we snooped around Mrs. Sam Oldenhaug's property, we'd have our answer.

"Look at it this way. Mrs. Thor Oldenhaug had insisted it didn't matter if we planted a bulb in honor of Mrs. Sam Oldenhaug since she wouldn't be attending the Memorial Day service anyway. Those two sisters-in-law have never gotten along, and I'll bet Mrs. Sam was so irked at Mrs. Thor that she decided to take a bulb when everyone was on the Peace Garden tour. She was the only one who didn't attend."

"And if I remember correctly," said Aunt Wilma, "her husband was killed in the Normandy Invasion. Maybe since she wasn't a charter Garden Club member and would receive no tribute for her hard work, she took the bulb to plant on her husband's grave as a tribute to him."

The next Sunday afternoon Shirley and Aunt Wilma drove to Hivdahl Cemetery. It was a long walk to the lilac bush at the east end. But there, growing beside a marker that read — Sam Oldenhaug, 1915 - 1944 — was a single Normandy Invasion Memorial Iris.

CHAPTER 5

THE CASE OF

The Fire at the Flickertail Lounge and Grill

The Fire at the Flickertail Lounge and Grill

Shirley and Ed were on their way to watch the Centennial Parade in Hivdahl and to visit Shirley's cousin Helen.

It seems only yesterday, thought Shirley, that Gloria Jean wore a pioneer dress and hat in the Kiddie Parade at the Jubilee Celebration.

"My, how time flies," she said aloud.

Ed, not knowing what she had been thinking, but annoyed at how late in the morning it was getting to be, said, "Well, it does when a person doesn't get going on time. I thought you'd never get out of that beauty parlor. I remember how the streets filled up for the last celebration, and if we don't allow plenty of time, we'll have to stand in the sun. If we have to do that, we'd be better off turning around right now and going home. Your Aunt Wilma was smart not wanting to come and stand in the heat and dust."

"But the Lord surely uses the heat in mysterious ways," said Shirley. "At the tent revival last month, everyone was sweating so profusely they all hurried up and converted so they could go home."

"Well, He could have the good sense to turn it off for a few days anyway," said Ed. "I doubt that heaven has a stuck thermostat."

Shirley knew Ed wasn't very happy. She had talked him into this Saturday excursion, and the fact that they didn't get going early enough made him even more sour.

Ed never liked to be late for anything, and when he had come into Martha's Beauty Parlour to pick her up, Shirley could tell he was impatient by the way he looked at his watch and jingled the change in his pocket.

As they drove, Shirley could feel herself getting more and more peeved. "You get worked up over the dumbest things, Ed. Martha is getting up in years and can't work as fast as she once did, especially since her knee surgery. In fact, I don't think there are too many her age who could work six days a week in her little cramped quarters behind the Flickertail. Poor thing has nothing to look at but the back of that hell hole of a liquor lounge Bud Schnitz runs. Now, if you'd quit looking at the fields and keep your eyes and mind on the road, I think we can get to Hivdahl by noon."

She knew her words wouldn't get Ed to speed up, but at least she had made the effort to get her point across.

Ed didn't say another word until they hit the outskirts of Hivdahl. "I hate driving in all this traffic. It's like a three-ring circus around here and just as hot and windy as it was at the celebration twenty-five years ago."

"Well, that's summer for you," sighed Shirley, tying a knot in the scarf under her chin. "At least it's not raining, so I don't have to worry about getting my hair wet just after having it fixed."

"We could use a few inches of rain," commented Ed as they pulled into Helen's driveway. "Now, we're not going to stay more than ten minutes, so be sure to let your cousin know that. Tell her we'll drink her coffee after the parade is over."

Shirley agreed, but she knew Helen would make them sit down for one quick cup and that Ed wouldn't say anything once he got inside her house.

Ed knew it too. It got on his nerves the way Helen had to control everything. He was convinced, though he had never mentioned it to Shirley, that Helen had driven her husband to an early grave.

The noon whistle blew just as they got out of the car, and seconds later the Heartsberg fire truck screamed down the street and turned onto the highway.

"It's bound to be a grass fire with this heat and wind," said Ed.

Shirley rang the doorbell. "What a shame our fire truck won't be in the parade."

Shirley and Ed declined seconds on the raisin molasses cookies and headed for Main Street. And when the news spread that Heartsberg's Flickertail Lounge and Grill was burning, Shirley wanted to leave immediately to see the damage and learn the facts. But since Ed seemed to be enjoying the festivities and had only come at her insistence, she didn't dare suggest it.

"You know, Ed," she said on the way home, "every Saturday morning when I get my hair fixed, a beer truck backs up to the back door of the Flickertail and unloads that barley silage. But this morning, there was no truck. Bud Schnitz was there though, wearing that awful white nylon shirt that doesn't begin to cover his beer belly. I remember Martha saying that unless the truck got there soon, Bud would miss it because he'd be on the way home for his noon meal."

Shirley had never spoken to Bud Schnitz, but she did know he hadn't been born or raised around Heartsberg. In fact, she had no idea where he came from. But that was typical of the owners of the Flickertail. Someone from out of town would buy the establishment, run it for a couple of years, then sell and move on. And someone else would continue the pattern.

Shirley and Ed could smell the smoke as they approached Heartsberg, but all they could see were charred remains and Bud Schnitz wringing his hands as he talked with the firemen.

Once home, Shirley called Aunt Wilma to see what she knew about the fire.

"Oh, Shirley," she said, "the smoke was so bad I stayed inside all afternoon with my windows shut. But I heard that no one was hurt. Frankly, I think the good Lord sees to it that dens of iniquity like the Flickertail burn down every once in awhile."

"I have news," said Ed on Monday morning when he returned from the post office with the mail. "The fire inspector thinks the fire may have started in the bathroom because of a short in the lightbulb cord. I also heard that Bud doesn't feel up to opening another lounge, so he will probably be moving out of town. And, Shirley, there is no reason for you to go to the Flickertail to poke around. It's roped off, and there are signs posted telling everyone to stay away."

"I have no intention of going," said Shirley to a surprised Ed. "But I wish the fire inspector would have talked to me first. I'd have pointed out some mighty interesting coincidences.

"Isn't it strange, Ed, that the fire began about noon, a time when Bud happened to be at home for lunch, and on a day when hardly a soul was left in town because of the big celebration in Hivdahl?

"And Martha and I are probably the only ones who knew that Bud didn't have any beer delivered that day? After all, why pay for something that you know is going to burn up?"

"Are you saying that Bud burned his own business to the ground?" asked Ed.

"It had to have been suffering with so many of his regulars saved at the tent revival," she answered. "And it stands to reason that if you can't make a living, one option is to burn your place down, collect the insurance, and move on. Anyway, a person who runs a business where the liquor flows obviously doesn't have much of a conscience."

"Bathroom fire?" laughed Ed. "That alibi really went to pot."

CHAPTER 6

THE CASE OF

The Edberg Boy Who Never Married

The Edberg Boy Who Never Married

Why the Edberg boy never married was not something many people cared about or gave a second thought to, but in the recesses of her mind, Shirley Holmquist knew there had to be some reason why Ray and Blanche's boy, Roy, had remained single.

It bothered her even more now that Roy had passed on, leaving his parents, who were getting up into their eighties, with all the milking and farming. Surely a clean, sensible man who had honorably served his country in World War II and had no visible mean streak in his bones would have had many chances to marry with all the Pederson and Swanson girls living in the same end of the township.

It was a cold November morning with snow lightly falling, and Shirley had no sooner walked into Benson & Benson Hardware when she heard Hardware Man Benson say to a dark-haired woman wearing a bright red coat and huge red earrings, "You'd be hard pressed to find a garlic press within 150 miles of here. As a matter of fact, I don't know if Grocer Jensen even carries garlic other than in pickling season. The people around here don't press it anyway. They just put it in the canning jars whole, the way God made it."

The woman thanked him in a strange-sounding accent and quickly walked out the door. Shirley and both Bensons looked out the window in time to see her get into Ray and Blanche Edberg's car.

"Well, I'll be," Mr. Benson muttered to Mrs. Benson and Shirley as he scratched his head. "I wonder where she blew in from."

Shirley didn't say anything. She knew enough to keep still in front of the Bensons because whatever she said was passed on to the next person who entered the store.

She had learned that the hard way. The previous December she had asked Mr. Benson if he knew why Grocer Jensen wasn't going to pass out free calendars for Christmas, and within the hour, Grocer Jensen called and said he would appreciate it if she would ask him why he wasn't giving out the calendars, instead of going through the busybody Bensons.

Shirley, home from the hardware store, was busy dusting her knick-knacks when Ed returned from the post office with the mail and the news that the Edbergs had a guest from Italy. Ole Axelson had told him it was a woman who planned to stay for a couple of weeks.

"So that was who I saw at Benson's this morning," said Shirley. "But how did Ray and Blanche get hooked up with her?"

"I don't know, I didn't ask, Ole Axelson didn't tell me, and I guess it's none of our business."

Well, that answered that, but Shirley remained puzzled. "Ed, they don't even go up North to the lakes in the summer, so how in the world would they know anyone from Italy?"

Ed didn't answer. He had mail to read, and he never felt he could answer her questions very satisfactorily anyway.

Shirley finished her dusting in a double quick hurry and went to see Aunt Wilma. Ray and Blanche Edberg, along with Aunt Wilma, had been three of the break-aways who had begun the Hope for the Living Word Lutheran Church after the '62 merger. Shirley was certain Aunt Wilma would have seen the Italian woman in church and would have information about her.

But Aunt Wilma didn't even know she existed. "The Edbergs weren't in church last Sunday at all. As a matter of fact, the last time I saw Mrs. Edberg was at Benson's Hardware a couple of weeks ago. She was buying silver polish, and I remember thinking how strange that was. Since they live so frugally, I didn't think she'd have much silver to polish, but maybe she was going to spiff things up for the Italian visitor."

"No, that can't be it," said Shirley. "Foreigners aren't usually that fussy, and Blanche wouldn't be the type to show off by using good silver even if she had it."

Aunt Wilma's eyes lit up. "Say, I know that Blanche's oldest sister who passed away several years ago used to be a missionary. I'll bet this lady is one of her missionary friends."

It didn't take long for Shirley to poke holes through that theory. "If she had been a missionary, Aunt Wilma, the Edbergs would have brought her to church to show slides. As far as I can see, the fact that they didn't even bring her to church means they're trying to hide something. Besides, Blanche's sister was a Lutheran missionary, and this lady is from Italy, which means she's a Catholic. So that just doesn't make sense."

But that night at supper, Ed said something to Shirley that did make sense and caused an idea to take root in her mind. However, she was more than a little peeved that Ed had never told her that when he worked in the post office, Roy had regularly gotten letters and packages from Italy.

Early the next morning she drove to the cemetery. Sure enough, there were footprints all around Roy Edberg's grave. Could it be that Roy had fallen in love while he was in Italy during the war, wondered Shirley. Poor man must have wanted to bring her home, but common sense told him she'd always be an outsider in Heartsberg. He probably died of a broken heart.

Shirley could hear the whistling teakettle as she rang Aunt Wilma's doorbell. And the two sat down to rusks and cups of steaming Postum.

"Do you think Roy kept his parents in the dark about her?" asked Aunt Wilma.

"I wouldn't be a bit surprised," replied Shirley. "But now that they know, they probably don't know how to explain the relationship, so that's why they didn't attend church last Sunday and bring the woman with them."

A frown furrowed Aunt Wilma's brow. "But I still don't understand why Mrs. Edberg was buying silver polish."

"That's easy," said Shirley. "The woman probably wrote the Edbergs, introduced herself, and asked if she could have some momentos of Roy. Since anything connected with farming would hold little meaning for her, she likely asked if she could have some of his war medals."

"I still don't understand," interrupted Aunt Wilma.

"Blanche probably didn't know how to say no, and since the Edbergs have no relatives who might someday want the medals, she decided to give them to her. But when she opened Roy's box and saw how tarnished they had become, she knew it would take more than soda to shine them up. And now, Aunt Wilma, I think we can let that matter rest in peace."

CHAPTER 7

THE CASE OF

The Anonymous Doorstep Donors

The Anonymous Doorstep Donors

"Just because the pastor said the money was an anonymous gift doesn't mean I'm not going to try to find out who gave it," said Shirley, giving Ed her how-dumb-can-you-be glare.

Ed knew there was no sense arguing with her, but he was upset enough to try. "I'm sure you feel like a dog who has just had a t-bone dangled in front of its eyes and then taken away. But as far as I am concerned, I don't care if I ever find out who gave the money to insure that the lutefisk suppers will continue. I am just thankful we're still going to have them. There were certainly far more important issues decided tonight," he said, turning on the television to catch the evening news.

The Holmquists had just returned from the annual meeting at First Lutheran of the Good Shepherd, and Shirley knew Ed was upset that two women had been elected to the church council. "They won't be happy until they have taken over the whole world," he muttered just loudly enough for Shirley to hear.

"You men didn't do such a hot job of picking out a new pastor, and you know it," Shirley reminded him. "I don't know how you can sit and complain about women being on the church council when you have never run for that office. Give them a chance, for crying out loud."

Ed knew he wasn't going to get anywhere in the argument, so he turned off the television and went to bed. Shirley knew it would be a long time before she would be able to fall asleep, so she began to think about what had transpired at the annual meeting.

Young Mrs. Ole Anderson had stood up and said, "This church should think about discontinuing lutefisk suppers. Everyone is so busy, and it's hard to find people to work. Besides, young people don't like lutefisk, and it's time the church moved forward instead of living in the past. You know, there are more than just Norwegians who belong to this church, and there are other things we can do to raise money for missions." (She was a Finn who had married a Norwegian, and some said she held it against her poor husband.) She sat down to a roomful of cold stares.

Then the Pastor had stood up. "Mrs. Ole Anderson and some other young members have told me how they feel about the lutefisk suppers. But I don't think we have any choice but to continue them. You see, on Saturday morning when I answered my doorbell, I saw two vistors standing there and a package lying on the step. When the visitors left, I opened it and found $2,000 in cash and a note saying that the money was to be used toward the purchase of food for the lutefisk supper. But there were three conditions listed: the supper must be served on a Friday instead of a Saturday; meatballs must be served along with lutefisk; and the proceeds must be given to foreign missions. The note also stated that the gift was to remain anonymous."

Shirley was getting sleepy, but not sleepy enough to give up her quest of finding out who the cash donor was. She pulled the church directory out of her nightstand and began paging through it.

The old man, Harold Odegaard, across the street, could have given the money. He had told Ed a month ago that he had heard rumors about some not wanting the lutefisk supper. And he was upset because, as he had told Ed, it was the only good thing left in the church after the merger.

But that man is so tight with his money, thought Shirley, that he'd never part with $2,000. She remembered how he had made his own crutches because he couldn't tolerate anyone charging such prices for a couple pieces of wood. Yet, he was still a possibility because he had threatened to join Stavanger Free Lutheran if the lutefisk suppers were discontinued.

Maybe it was one of the Opdahls from east of town. Most of them had married Catholics, and maybe they wanted to insure that there would be at least one bona fide fish dinner the whole family could attend. Moving it to Friday would satisfy the requirements for the Catholic spouses, and serving lutefisk would satisfy the older Opdahl's Norwegian pride. And the young ones would attend because there would be something more than lutefisk to eat. They had money too, Shirley reminded herself.

Suddenly Ed tapped her on the shoulder. "Don't you know it's 4:30 in the morning? Pretty soon it will be time to get up."

Shirley decided to stay up and get an early start on the wash.

Later that morning she called Aunt Wilma and told her what had transpired at the annual meeting. Aunt Wilma, who had left First Lutheran of the Good Shepherd when it voted to merge, rather enjoyed hearing — though she never let on to Shirley — that the congregation had a few problems.

"Sounds like there's a Catholic connection," she said, "or a sour-graped Swede."

Shirley was stung by Aunt Wilma's phrase. She and Aunt Wilma were 100% Norwegian, but Shirley had married Ed, a full-blooded Swede. Even though she had reminded Aunt Wilma over the years that there really wasn't any difference between Norwegians and Swedes except that Swedes were a bit more stubborn, held grudges longer, and preferred hardtack to lefse and cream sauce to butter on their lutefisk, Aunt Wilma had never bought Shirley's viewpoint and occasionally liked to get in her digs.

Shirley was relieved when Ed walked in with the mail. Aunt Wilma was getting on her nerves, and it gave her an excuse to get off the phone.

"I heard that the $2,000 left on the pastor's doorstep was all in $1.00 bills, and some of them were very old," said Ed.

A mattress stuffer, thought Shirley, as she poured Ed a cup of morning coffee. She wanted more information, but she didn't ask because she knew from experience that a wrong question from her could get Ed to completely clam up on a subject.

All week long Shirley thought about the anonymous gift of money. Either Ed didn't know or else simply didn't offer any new information, and things weren't coming together as she had hoped. Several times she had told Aunt Wilma, "It may take a good long time to figure out this mystery."

But on Saturday when the Solbergsogndahl sisters came to the Holmquist's door with their weekly egg delivery, Shirley cracked the case.

"And," she explained to Aunt Wilma later that day, "I don't know why I never thought of them. It just makes sense. No one likes potlucks and church suppers more than those two women. They haven't missed one in years. They even go to funerals of people they hardly know just for the lunch and fellowship. I remember Ed saying once that a person never had to worry that the church would be empty for his funeral because the Solbergsogndahl sisters would always show up.

"There's more evidence, too," she continued. "Who else would have $2,000 in one dollar bills lying around the house except someone who was collecting them on a regular basis?"

"You're right," said Aunt Wilma. "Most of the people I know have bought two-dozen-for-a-dollar eggs from them for years."

"And the year I was chairman of the lutefisk supper, I remember one of the sisters asking why we never served Swedish meatballs with the lutefisk as we had years before," said Shirley. "Their mother was Swedish, you know. And," she added with special emphasis, "they turned out to be two of the hardest working mission-minded women anyone could ever meet. I'll bet they were the two visitors at the pastor's door with their

Saturday egg delivery. They probably set down the package of money, rang the doorbell, and waited for him to come. That way they knew their money would be safe."

"It makes sense to me. I told you it must be either a Catholic or a sour-graped Swede," said Aunt Wilma, getting in a final dig.

But Shirley, not to be outdone, replied, "Well, it wasn't a Catholic. The Solbergsogndahl sisters must have wanted it on Friday because they're so busy delivering eggs on Saturday, they'd be too tuckered out to enjoy the meal. And, Aunt Wilma, I'll bet every congregation wishes they had two sour-graped Swedes as generous as those two women."

CHAPTER 8

THE CASE OF

The Lutefisk Heist

The Lutefisk Heist

It was lefse baking day for Shirley and Aunt Wilma. Shirley was rolling, Aunt Wilma was frying, and they were working up a storm until Ed came home from the post office with the mail and some mighty shocking news.

He didn't even bother to take his hat off before breaking the story. "Ole Axelson's Meat Market was broken into last night, and somebody made off with three of his four barrels of lutefisk and nearly two pounds of Swedish meatball mix."

He bent down and unbuckled his overshoes. "And that's not the half of it. About an hour ago when the sheriff was at Ole's store writing up the crime report, a call came over his radio that the meat market in Bergendale had been hit too. They'd cleaned house there, taking three barrels of lutefisk plus a jar of beef jerky. I hear Ole is pretty shook up, and I can't blame him. Those barrels of fish had been reserved for the Stavanger Free Lutheran lutefisk dinner this weekend, and Ole can't get any more until the delivery truck comes on Monday. Poor guy doesn't know which way to turn."

"Who could have done it? What evidence was there?" asked Shirley, as she continued to roll her dough.

"Not much," admitted Ed. "Some say that by the looks of the tire tracks, the get-away vehicle was a Ford pick-up with bald tires. But no one can be positive because it snowed all night, and the tracks are pretty covered up."

Aunt Wilma had been listening intently. "Well, I don't know about you," she said, "but I think since we've already paid for our tickets to the lutefisk feed and there is only one barrel of fish to go around, we'd better be at Stavanger Free Lutheran when the doors open or we won't even get to smell the fish."

But Shirley's mind wasn't on the lutefisk dinner. It was the crime that intrigued her. And even though she knew Ed wouldn't like her idea, she said, "I was just thinking this morning that I should go to Ole's Meat Market and get some pork chops and head cheese. He is running a good sale this week."

She was right. Ed didn't like her idea. "You can go there tomorrow," he said. "It's best we wait until things settle down so we don't look like we're prying or interferring in the official investigation."

Shirley didn't answer. Well, he can wait until tomorrow, she thought, but after we finish this lefse, I'm going to take Aunt Wilma home and then swing by Ole's just to see what's up."

She didn't dare go into the store since she knew Ed would find out and get mad. But there was no harm in looking, she told herself, as she drove slowly down the alley behind the store.

There wasn't much to see except some snow-covered tire tracks and one set of footprints to the left of the store's back door. Then she noticed a horizontal slice in the fluffy snow. It looked as if someone had cut into a piece of meringue. She hurriedly drove out of the alley. She didn't want to be gone too long or Ed would surely suspect she was up to something.

The next morning Aunt Wilma called to say that the lutefisk feed was on hold for another week. Shirley cut the conversation short because she could see Ed coming up the driveway, and she wanted to know what news he had learned at the post office.

"It's a bigger case than we ever thought," he began excitedly, as he stamped his overshoes on the rag rug. "There's talk the sheriff might call in the F.B.I. since the lutefisk is probably destined for the black market out East. The thieves will no doubt sell it on the streets of Brooklyn. There's a big Norwegian settlement out there, you know, and those people are so used to buying from peddlers and street vendors, they wouldn't be one bit suspicious."

He caught his breath. "And then the veterinarian in Bergendale was robbed last night. So, with drugs in the picture, the Mafia might be involved. Tonight the sheriff and two deputies are going to be parked on the highway east of town checking cars with out-of-state license plates.

"Honestly, Shirley, big city crime has come to Heartsberg. Ole is offering a hind quarter of beef to anyone who can point the finger at the criminals. One thing is for sure, I'm putting deadbolts on our doors. It's not safe here anymore."

"Ed, don't get so worked up," said Shirley. "And

before you start putting any locks on, I'm going to Ole's Meat Market to get my pork chops and head cheese and to check out something. I'll be back within the hour to tell you who committed the crime."

It took her less than twenty minutes.

"Ed," she said teasingly, "I think you should go to Ole's and collect the reward. With Gloria Jean and Merle coming for Christmas, and you know the way that husband of hers eats, we could use the extra meat."

She poured two cups of coffee and continued. "Right away I knew it wasn't an outside job. No one from New York would be dumb enough to drive all the way out here when the lutefisk could be hoisted right off the docks when it arrived from Norway. Besides, if they drove all the way to New York, the two pounds of meatball mix would spoil.

"The thieves were not only familiar with Ole's Meat Market, but also with the one in Bergendale and the veterinarian's office there. So I reasoned that they lived halfway between the two towns. And think about it, Ed. Those barrels of lutefisk are too heavy for anyone to steal just for the fun of it. And no one in his right mind could eat that much. So the lutefisk must have been desperately needed for something.

"Who's hurting the most around here? The pig farmers. Pork hasn't been this cheap in years. Some honest people will become dishonest just to keep from going belly-up. If they can't afford to feed their pigs, and if they know they aren't going to get much when they sell them, they might stoop to stealing food for them."

Ed added another sugar lump to his coffee.

"You remember, Ed, those brothers who moved up from Iowa and rented the old Ingebretson farm south of town to raise pigs? That's halfway between here and Bergendale. The word is that they stick to themselves and don't like to neighbor. Well, I know they drive a Ford pick-up because I've seen them in town. And I can well imagine they wouldn't have enough money to buy new tires if theirs were bald."

"And I guess no one would start driving to New York with bald tires either," conceded Ed.

Shirley went on. "As I drove down the alley behind Ole's store on the day of the crime (Shirley knew Ed wouldn't like to hear this, but she counted on his being so wrapped up in her story, he'd forget he had told her to stay away), I saw tire tracks, foot prints, and a good-sized horizontal slice in the snow by the door. I think the pick-up was backed to the door. Then the brother on the passenger side got out, pulled out a ramp that left the slice in the snow, and rolled the lutefisk barrels up the ramp. Then, on impulse, he grabbed the meatball mix for their dinner, and then they made a quick getaway."

"But why did they only take three barrels and leave the fourth?" asked Ed.

"I've looked at Merle's pick-up enough to know that it can only hold three barrels," said Shirley. "And this morning I verified that when I got a good look at the size of Ole's remaining barrel."

Ed was puzzled. "You think the brothers fed the lutefisk to their pigs?"

"Yes, and the pigs must have gotten so sick, the brothers could either watch them die or steal medicine from the veterinarian."

Ed just shook his head. "Well," he said, "I think it's my duty to bring the sheriff over here so you can tell him about this. But don't think for one minute I'm going to collect that hind quarter of beef from Ole. He's had more than his share of tough luck this week without my trying to capitalize on it."

CHAPTER 9

THE CASE OF

The Forbidden Fruit

The Forbidden Fruit

Shirley's Circle had spent the better part of the morning bagging goodies for the Sunday School children. At First Lutheran of the Good Shepherd, it was a tradition to give each child who participated in the Christmas program a bag containing an apple, a variety of nuts — almonds, walnuts, hazels, pecans, peanuts — and a few pieces of hard holiday candy.

The women had organized an assembly line so they could clip along at a good pace. Mrs. Andrew Olson opened the brown paper bags and set them on end. Mrs. G.J. Jensen put two scoops of nuts into each bag. The pastor's wife polished the apples, and Mrs. Lester Olavness put them in the bags. Miss Olive Thorson shoveled in two scoops of candy, and since Mrs. Emil Strandquist was sick, Shirley did double duty. She cut the ribbon that was to be tied around each bag, tied a bow, and then curled the ribbon ends with the edge of a scissors.

"I don't know about you," said Miss Olive Thorson, "but when I was a child, we were a lot more appreciative of the treats the church gave us at Christmas than these kids are. We didn't get as many nuts as they do either."

"It gets worse every year," chimed in Mrs. G.J. Jensen, as she put a scoop of nuts into a bag. "If their attitudes don't change, I think we should just eliminate treats altogether."

"Well," said Shirley, "when I saw four smashed apples outside the church after last year's program, I was thinking the same thing. But, you know, kids nowadays eat apples and nuts for snacks, so this is no special treat for them. Maybe we should just bag them up for the shut-ins instead."

The pastor's wife, who hadn't said much since she came, spoke up. "I think it's a good idea to give some special treats to our shut-ins, but I don't think apples or nuts are very appropriate. Most of them don't have the teeth to handle that kind of food. Maybe we could give them cheese or peach sauce."

Shirley was irked. She was sure none of the women wanted to spend more money on the shut-ins, but no one dared disagree with the pastor's wife. Well, she wasn't about to let that idea stand without comment.

"As far as the shut-ins go, it's the thought that counts," she said, as she continued to cut, tie, and curl the ribbon. "I know they don't expect us to support them."

The pastor and his wife had only been in Heartsberg for two months, and although Shirley knew it was only fair to reserve judgment until they had been in town for at least six, she didn't feel they were the same caliber folk as the previous pastor and his wife. Aunt Wilma had told her many times that liberal seminary training made new, young pastors a different breed. Shirley wasn't sure she completely agreed with that, though. It seemed to her that pastors' wives had changed more than the pastors.

Years ago pastors' wives wouldn't have dreamed of

picking out their own wallpaper and paint for the parsonage. They were always satisfied with whatever the church council decided. But this pastor's wife not only dismissed every rule and regulation in the congregational by-laws entitled *"The Care and Feeding of the Pastor and his Family,"* she also let the council know she needed soft water. Can you beat that! Twenty-five years ago the pastor's wife was just thankful to have running water.

There were other things, too, that didn't set right with Shirley. Not one soul, not even the council members, had been invited to the parsonage for an open house and tour. Miss Olive Thorson had mentioned that she had seen the pastor's wife entertaining her kids with Tic-Tac-Toe and Hangman on the back of the Sunday bulletin in the middle of the pastor's sermon. And others had commented that she talked more about the secular than the sacred things in life.

Shirley was relieved when they finally finished bagging the Sunday School treats, and she felt even better when the pastor's wife said she couldn't come the next day to help fill the food baskets for the shut-ins. One bad apple spoils the whole bunch, she said to herself.

But when the Circle members gathered in the church basement, there wasn't a leftover apple or nut to be found anywhere. "What a shame," lamented Shirley. "I guess the shut-ins will have to be satisfied with cookies this year." But she knew she couldn't be satisfied until she knew all the facts.

When she told Ed about the missing apples and

nuts, he said, "It must have been the kids." Shirley was positive he was wrong. She knew kids well enough to realize that if they were going to steal, they'd go for pop or candy. She hated to think the pastor's wife would stoop so low, but her comments questioning the wisdom of giving apples and nuts to the shut-ins made Shirley wonder.

"Aunt Wilma," she said over the phone that evening. "If you had seen the way the pastor's wife looked at the apples when she was polishing them yesterday, you'd have to think she might have pulled an Eve and taken the forbidden fruit. She might be the kind of pastor's wife who thinks that any food left at the church automatically becomes the property of the pastor."

"I've heard there are pastors' wives who feel that way," said Aunt Wilma. "A few years ago one over in Hivdahl got caught taking the pennies out of a birthday bank."

Shirley couldn't wait until the next evening. She and Ed were going to bring a couple of chickens to the parsonage as a Christmas gift for the pastor and his family. In years past, it had just been Ed who delivered them. But since she hadn't seen the parsonage, and it would give her the chance to ask the pastor right in front of his wife if he knew what had happened to the leftover apples and nuts, she made plans to go.

They arrived when the family was eating supper, and Shirley could sense that Ed was uncomfortable and wanted to make it a short visit. So she plunged in. "Pastor, do you know what happened to the leftover apples and nuts?"

"I wasn't even aware there had been any apples or nuts left," he answered.

When Shirley glanced at the pastor's wife to see if she were reacting in a guilty way, her eyes fell on a flowered china bowl in the center of the table. Waldorf salad. It was so chocked full of apples and nuts she could hear them crunch as the pastor's wife put a forkful into her mouth.

Shirley didn't need any further evidence. "Ed," she said on the way home, "No one serves Waldorf salad for everyday unless they're rich, and even though we pay the pastor pretty well for what he does, it still isn't enough for them to indulge in a salad like that at an ordinary meal."

The next Sunday the pastor's wife and children sat down in the pew ahead of Shirley and Ed. And Shirley knew she'd have a hard time mustering up a polite hello when they shook hands during the Peace. Ed had never felt comfortable shaking hands during the service, and now she knew exactly how he felt.

Shirley was thinking about the missing apples and nuts when the pastor started his sermon — *Give and It Shall Be Given Unto You.* But she was jolted back to attention when he began telling a story.

"Last Christmas," he said, "when my family was eating supper, a dirty, tattered man whom I had never seen before, stopped at our house. He was driving a rusty, dilapidated car full of kids. And he asked if he could borrow $2.00 for gas because he was broke and on his way North to try to get work.

"I gave him the money and a bag of groceries," the

pastor continued. "And even though he said he'd pay me back, I never expected to hear from him again.

"Well, one night last week as we were having family devotions, there was a knock at the door. There he stood, the same man, carrying a bushel of apples and a big bag of mixed nuts. He had looked long and hard to find our new residence, but he wanted to say thanks for the kindness. He had found a good job and was once again on his feet."

Shirley didn't want to hear any more. She was ashamed. The circumstantial evidence had seemed overwhelming, but it had been wrong, and she had jumped to a petty conclusion.

She felt even more humbled when, during the Peace, the pastor's wife looked her straight in the eyes and said, "My husband found out that when the Luther Leaguers went caroling, they passed out the leftover apples and nuts to the needy."

But the worst sting came from Ed. He gave her a "see-I-didn't-figure-you-were-right" nudge and then whispered, "Didn't I tell you it was the kids?"

CHAPTER 10

THE CASE OF

The Telltale Slop Pail

The Telltale Slop Pail

People in Heartsberg usually died at home or in the hospital in a peaceful manner with their hands folded and a *Reader's Digest* or a devotional book tented over their chests.

A few residents, notably teenagers, had died in tragic automobile accidents, and two had been killed when tractors overturned on them, but no one in Heartsberg had ever been murdered. Elmo Martinson said he had once seen someone push a transient off the Soo Line, but since no one knew the man, the sheriff just buried him.

Usually in the spring or right after a hard frost, about four or five Heartsbergians would be called Home. There seemed to be something about the change of seasons that triggered the deaths.

One spring morning, Shirley received a call from Ingeborg Bjornson, the president of her Circle.

"Ida Iverson slept away last night," said Ingeborg. "A person never knows. Mrs. Ole Severson found her when she went to her house this morning to go for a walk with her."

"I suppose it was her time," said Shirley. But she was surprised. Two days ago the only thing Ida had complained about was a little arthritis in her knee.

"Poor thing doesn't have any relatives around here,"

continued Ingeborg. "Her closest cousin in Hivdahl will come this afternoon, but she wondered if someone from Ida's Circle would watch the house until she arrives. I'd go, but I have a doctor's appointment in fifteen minutes."

"I'll go right away, Ingeborg. That's the least I can do," said Shirley.

She hurriedly called Aunt Wilma and gave her the details. "And could you come and keep me company? I knew Ida, but not that well that I'd want to sit in her house by myself."

"Sure," said Aunt Wilma. "I'm not doing anything that can't wait until tomorrow anyway."

The hearse was just pulling away from Ida's house as Shirley and Aunt Wilma turned onto Maple Street.

"They don't waste much time," said Shirley. "I thought we'd at least get a look at her."

Even though she wasn't much to look at, Ida was a lovely person. She had never married, but Shirley thought it was because she was so fussy and nervous.

Aunt Wilma had never married either, but that was different. She was the youngest in her family and was so busy taking care of her aged parents, there was no time for romance. By the time they died, the years had slipped by, and it was too late. "I guess it was just my lot in life," she had told Shirley many times.

"Looks as though Ida was expecting company," said Aunt Wilma, as they walked into the dining room and saw two place settings of china, Fostoria, and sterling silverware.

"You know Ida," said Shirley, turning over a cup to

see what kind it was. "She probably wasn't going to have company until next week, but she liked to get things done ahead of time and not be rushed. By the looks of the doilies and mop boards, she had already finished her spring housecleaning too."

"Maybe that's why she died," said Aunt Wilma. "It was probably getting to be too much for her."

"I'm going to get some coffee cooked before Ida's cousin gets here, or she's going to wonder what we've been doing," said Shirley as she started hunting through the kitchen cupboards.

"I can get these dishes done while you make the coffee," said Aunt Wilma.

"Dishes? Now that's strange. No matter how sick she felt, Ida would never have left dirty dishes in the sink," puzzled Shirley as she looked at the unwashed plate, cup, knife, fork, and spoon.

"Why, it looks as though there has been ketchup on the plate," said Aunt Wilma.

"I think we'd better find out what Ida had been eating," said Shirley, and she reached underneath the sink and lifted the cover of the slop pail.

"Something's rotten in Denmark!" she exclaimed, gazing at two pork chop bones and some kernels of corn.

Both women knew it hadn't been Ida who had eaten the pork chops and corn. She was too old to digest corn, and as she had told the Circle on numerous occasions, "The book of Leviticus forbids God's people to eat pork, so who am I to argue?"

"I'm getting goose bumps," said Aunt Wilma,

rubbing her arms. "I hope Ida's cousin gets here soon."

"Just pour yourself some coffee and try to relax, Aunt Wilma. I'm going to check the broom closet and back porch to make sure we're alone."

Shirley and Aunt Wilma were only too eager to leave when Ida's cousin arrived. At the door Aunt Wilma turned and said sympathetically, "I'm glad Ida died peacefully."

"I don't know how peacefully she died," said Shirley as they walked to the car. "But I can't quite put my finger on what happened."

Early the next morning Shirley was at Aunt Wilma's door.

"I thought about it half the night," she said. "I'll bet Ida was a sucker for traveling peddlers. She didn't have the heart to say no, so she invited them in and bought whatever they were selling."

"I don't understand," said Aunt Wilma, a frown etching her forehead.

"Yesterday I noticed that Ida had two fairly new sets of encyclopedias. Why would a person her age have two sets unless she had been pressured into buying them? There was also a brand new Kirby vacuum cleaner in the broom closet. Now, that would have been way too heavy for her to maneuver. And with all the knives in the kitchen drawer, she could have opened a restaurant."

Aunt Wilma was deep in thought. "I remember Mrs. Severson saying once that Ida had enough cancer insurance to cover the whole county."

"Well," continued Shirley, "I remembered how Miss Olive Thorson had told the Altar Guild that she bought a set of pots and pans from a persistent peddler. He had made an appointment to cook dinner at her house so she could see how well the kettles worked.

"Dollars to doughnuts, that salesman was at Ida's house when she died. He must have made the same appointment with her, so she set her dining room table for two. But when she realized pork chops were on the menu, she didn't know how to say she didn't eat the stuff, so she went upstairs to lie down. The more she thought about eating pork, the more upset she became, until, finally, she just had a heart attack."

"I imagine," broke in Aunt Wilma, "that she was also pretty worn out from all her spring housecleaning."

"That too," agreed Shirley. "Then when Ida didn't come for dinner, and the salesman realized she was dead and he wouldn't make a sale, he decided to eat the dinner and take off. He probably hadn't eaten all day, and you know how hungry men get. Anyway, he got a plate, cup, and silverware from her cupboard, some ketchup from the refrigerator, sat down and ate. He had some coffee too, because when I got the cream from the refrigerator for Ida's cousin's coffee, I noticed from the line on the side of the pitcher, that someone had used it.

"When he finished eating, he dumped the scraps in the slop pail, gathered up his pots and pans, and left. Didn't you think it was strange, Aunt Wilma, that Ida had dirty dishes, but no dirty pots and pans?"

Aunt Wilma hadn't thought about that, but everything Shirley was saying made sense. "You know," she said, "Mrs. Severson called this morning to say the coroner's report indicated that Ida died about 5:00 p.m."

"Oh, I knew it couldn't have happened much before 5:00," said Shirley, "because when I opened her refrigerator, I saw that she had changed baking soda boxes yesterday. She had written '3-2-88, 4:00 p.m.' on the new one."

"Are you going to report this?" asked Aunt Wilma.

"Goodness, no," said Shirley. "I'm sure the salesman is long gone, and besides, there was no foul play involved."

She refilled the coffee cups. "Scripture says some strangers might be angels, but, Aunt Wilma, let this be a lesson to you. Unless the stranger is the Watkins man or the pastor, don't let him take a step inside your door."

CHAPTER 11

THE CASE OF

The Laundry That Came Up Short

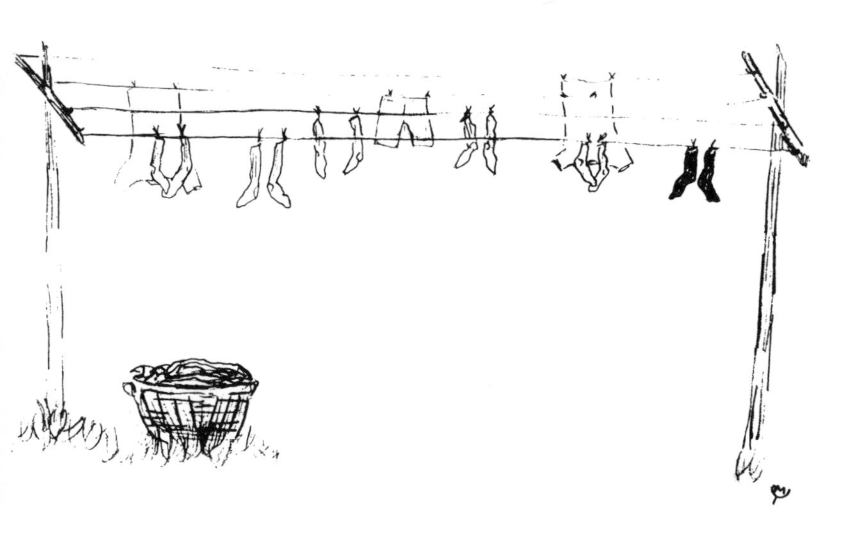

The Laundry That Came Up Short

It was Monday, wash day, and Shirley was busy trying to get the clean clothes folded and put away before she had to start making dinner. Ed liked to eat exactly at 12:00 noon. He had told Shirley many times that the reason Heartsberg blew a noon whistle was to let people know it was time to eat.

As Shirley put Ed's clean white socks in the drawer, she realized there were only five pairs instead of the usual six. That's not right, she said to herself as she went down the basement and checked to see if the other socks had been left in the washer.

They hadn't. And they weren't lying beside the clothes line outside either.

"Well, I've heard people say that washing machines eat socks, but this is the first time it has happened to me," she said to Ed as she set some cold roast beef sandwiches and leftover salad on the table.

"It's nothing to get upset about," he said. "You can just buy another pair."

"The point is," Shirley said, "that I buy you six pairs of white socks at the same time, one for each work day, so they will all wear out at the same time. That way I don't have to wonder how long each will hold up."

Ed finished eating and turned on the radio to listen to the weather report and record the barometric pressure. He had been doing it for years. "Looks like the summer of '36," he said. "The top soil is blowing off like the dust bowl, and there's no rain in sight."

Shirley's mind was still on the missing socks. "If you're out and about this afternoon, Ed, maybe you could ask around and see if anyone has seen them. Maybe they blew away this morning, but I'm always very careful to secure them well with the clothespins."

"Don't be ridiculous," said Ed. "I'm not going to ask if anyone has seen my white socks. They might get the wrong idea and think I'm accusing them of stealing. Maybe some kids took them. You hang that laundry out so early in the morning, it's still dark. Anyone could walk through the yard and take them and never be seen."

Shirley had to admit she started her wash plenty early in the morning. Her mother had been that way too. "The earlier the better," she had always counseled Shirley.

Shirley had a lot of extra work that needed to be done that week because Gloria Jean, Merle, and Mary Jane were coming to visit.

They always came to Heartsberg for the county fair. Merle's brother raced in the stock car derby, and Merle's entire family wouldn't miss the races for love nor money. Cars were their life, and, as Shirley had warned Gloria Jean before she married, "You'll have to learn to live with it because the whole family has car fever in their blood."

Gloria Jean didn't go to the races, but she enjoyed

the 4-H exhibits. So did Shirley. They had both worked hard in 4-H, and that's where Gloria Jean had learned most of her homemaking skills.

Mary Jane loved the fair because, as Shirley saw it, she got to do everything and buy everything she wanted. She'd ride on all the rides she could stand, waste money like crazy trying to win a gaudy teddy bear or dancing hula girl on a stick, and eat junk food until she'd get sick. Shirley didn't approve, but what could she say?

When Gloria Jean and her family arrived, Shirley told her right away about the missing pair of socks. "I can't for the life of me understand what happened to them, but then I guess there are a lot of things that go on nowadays that I don't understand."

Gloria Jean knew her mother well enough to recognize the comment as an indirect critique on how she and Merle were raising Mary Jane.

"Forget about it, Mom," she said. "Let's go to the fair."

"All right," said Shirley, "but there are some things in life a person can't forget."

I can't win, thought Gloria Jean. Mom will never let me forget that I married Merle against her wishes and moved to the Cities, which is, as as she has pointed out dozens of times, no place to raise a family.

Mary Jane insisted they hit the Midway right away. Gloria Jean said that was fine with her, but she knew Shirley was upset. She remembered Merle's words as they drove into the Holmquist's driveway, "You can be nice to your mother without letting her run all over you." She had given him a hug and said, "That's easier said than done."

Mary Jane was having the time of her life. Shirley and Gloria Jean watched her spin and whirl and dip until Shirley said, "I think you've had enough. I'm getting dizzy just watching you."

"Just one more ride," begged Mary Jane. "I want to go on the Octopus."

And she got her way. As Shirley looked in disgust at the greasy, dirty-looking, tattooed man who was taking the tickets and running the ride, she happened to look at his feet.

"Gloria Jean," she whispered. "I'm sure those are Ed's missing socks he's wearing. Aunt Wilma says people always lose things when the fair comes to town."

"Don't be foolish," said Gloria Jean. "Millions of people own white socks, and there is no way under the sun you can tell Dad's socks from anyone else's."

"Oh yes there is," said Shirley, as she stared at the man's feet. "I sew E.H., Ed's initials, in red thread on the bottom of his socks right by the toes, and I think I see some red threads poking through that man's sandals."

The Octopus operator had been eyeing them warily. "Got a problem?" he asked sarcastically, taking a Lucky Strike from his mouth.

The tone of his voice set Shirley off. "I think you stole my husband's socks," she said in a stern voice.

"Look, lady," he said, showing her his rotted-out little teeth. "I'm warning you, get out of here before you're sorry."

Gloria Jean grabbed Mary Jane, took her mother by the arm, and hurried them away as fast as she could. "I don't believe it, Mother," she said. "A lousy pair of socks.

I just don't believe it. We're going home."

In the car Shirley begged Gloria Jean not to tell Ed what had happened. "I'll forget it," she said, "if you will."

Ed was watching television. "I'm glad you're back," he said. "I've been thinking about those socks."

Gloria Jean rolled her eyes and said under her breath, "I just don't believe this is happening."

Ed continued, "We went to Ida Iverson's funeral on Thursday, and I wore my dark Sunday socks on that day. So, rightfully, there should have been only five pairs of white socks in the wash."

"That's a relief," said Shirley. "But then I should have washed two pairs of Sunday socks."

"Naw," said Ed. "They weren't that dirty so I put them back in my drawer and wore them again on Sunday. I think sometimes you just wash clothes for the sake of washing, whether they're dirty or not."

"I'll say amen to that," Gloria Jean said. "But I've got a question, Mom. Why do you sew Dad's initials on the bottom of his socks?"

"I've always done it," Shirley answered. "If your dad ever had to go to the hospital in a hurry, I'd never get the right ones back if they weren't marked."

Gloria Jean winked at her. "I wonder if that's why the Octopus operator does it too."

CHAPTER 12

THE CASE OF

The Cool-Headed Claim Jumper

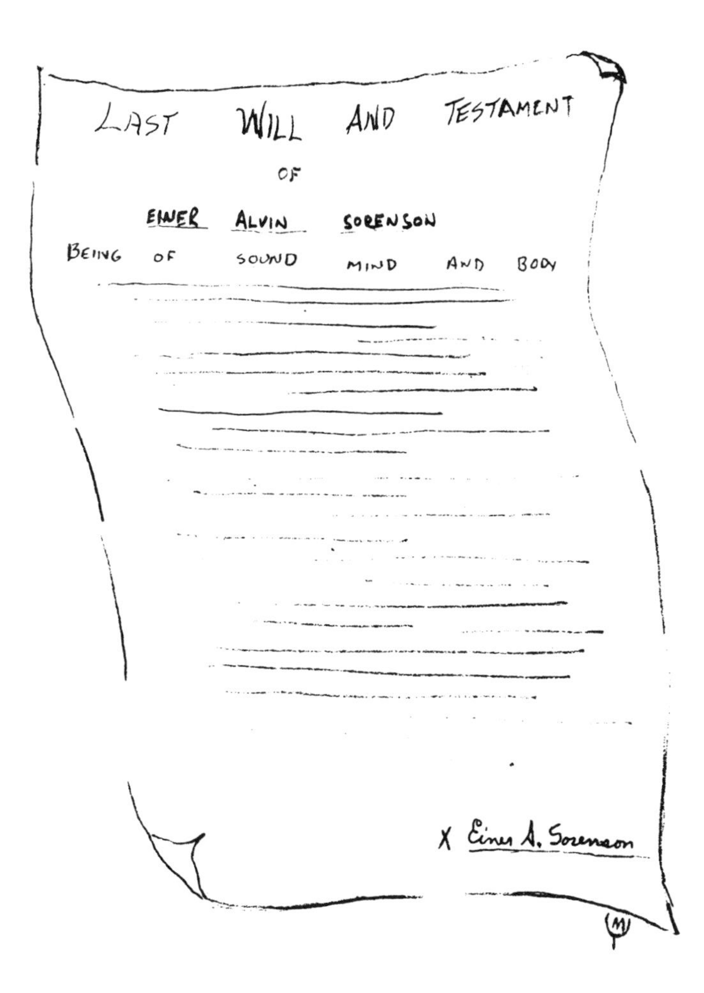

The Cool-Headed Claim Jumper

It was the time of year when tulips and daffodils push through the heavy cold dirt, the birds return from the South, the farmers gear up for planting, and Heartsbergians lose another citizen or two from their fair community.

Ida Iverson wasn't even cold when Ed returned from the post office with the news that Einar Sorenson had been found dead, crumpled on the floor of his kitchen, clutching a bottle of heart pills.

Before he could finish detailing the account, Signe Svendahl appeared at the door.

"As soon as I heard of Einar's tragedy," she said, "I thought I'd do the neighborly thing and call his grandniece in the Cities with the news. She was his only relative and his namesake, you know, and I found her number in Einar's little directory right beside his phone."

"That was thoughtful," said Shirley. "The few times I had a conversation with Einar, he spoke so highly of Eleanore and her good job at Lutheran headquarters."

"But this is the strange part, Shirley," continued Signe. "Eleanore can't come to Heartsberg for a few days, so she asked if I would make the funeral arrangements. Now, I've only seen the woman once, and that was from a distance. And she certainly doesn't know me. I tried to tell her that, but she said to just go ahead."

"That is odd, but I'll be glad to help you with the arrangements," said Shirley, ignoring Ed's stay-out-of-it look. "Let's start right away. Einar hadn't been to church for so long, I don't know if we'll be able to find a decent funeral suit."

"I wonder why he never came to church," said Signe. "He looked like a Christian."

"He acted like one too," said Shirley. "But then, none of us knew him very well. He lived on the farm for so long by himself that when he retired to town, I guess he never felt comfortable socializing."

"This place belonged to a bachelor, all right," said Signe, as the women walked through the rooms of his tiny house. "But it looks as though he did keep it picked up."

Shirley pulled a suit from the closet and breathed a sigh of relief. She also found clean underwear without holes in a dresser drawer and Einar's good black shoes under the bed.

"I'm going to give them a quick coat of polish," she told Signe who was checking the refrigerator.

"I just wanted to see if Einar had been eating decently, or if something here caused him to die," she said, looking at moldy gammelost, a jar of buttermilk, two crusts of rye bread, four eggs, and a pound of old-looking venison. "Fy da! You can tell there wasn't a woman cooking here."

Shirley was shuffling papers on Einar's desk. "By the

looks of his bank statement, there will be a great plenty to pay for the funeral and then some. Too bad Einar wasn't active in the church. We could have used some more money in the Memorial Fund since it was drained to buy the new hymnals. Now, Signe, this is interesting. The last check to Eleanore was written on January 25, and it hasn't cleared the bank yet."

But Signe was entranced by the photograph on the desk top. "Look at this, Shirley," she said. "Einar must have treasured this picture of the two of them. What a happy, smiling child Eleanore was."

"And you can certainly tell they were family," said Shirley. "Their jaws are the same, strong and square."

On their way home, Shirley and Signe stopped at First Lutheran of the Good Shepherd to discuss the service with the pastor and the funeral home where they picked out a moderately priced casket that matched Einar's coloring. Once home, Shirley called Ingeborg Bjornson, her Circle president, to arrange for the lunch following the service.

"There won't be too many people," she said, "just one relative and then the regulars, maybe fifty-two at the most."

Signe thanked Shirley for all her help and went home.

"There is a lot to planning a funeral," Shirley told Ed. "I've been at it all day."

"Well, it looks as though you enjoyed every minute of it," he replied, sitting down to the cold supper she had hastily put on the table.

On the day of the funeral, Shirley and Signe left early

to talk with Eleanore. But when they tried to enter Einar's driveway, they were waved off by a husky woman with bushy blond hair, dressed entirely in bright purple — dress, hoop earrings, nylons, and shoes — who was hoisting furniture onto the back of a pick-up.

"Neiman, uff da," muttered Shirley. "Would Lutheran headquarters hire someone like that?"

"Well," said Signe, watching her lift a brass floor lamp, "we'd better go talk to her."

But Eleanore was not anxious to talk. She was polite, but quite cold as she thanked them for their help and said she'd handle everything else. "I have to get back to the Cities tonight," she said, pitching a desk atop the heap, "so I really don't have time to stand here talking."

"I've never seen a woman drive to a funeral in a pick-up," said Shirley, as they drove away, "much less a relative of the deceased."

Shirley, Ed, Aunt Wilma, and Signe sat in the third pew, and Eleanore sat alone in the first. Shirley noticed that she didn't once take out a hanky to wipe her eyes or blow her nose.

Over lunch in the basement, Aunt Wilma whispered, "Look at her huge purple ring. It doesn't seem appropriate to be so gaudy at a funeral."

"My goodness," interrupted Signe, "is she already leaving? Some people haven't gotten through the lunch line yet."

"I don't like the looks of this," said Shirley. "I'm going to follow her."

"I'm going to walk home," said Ed. "I see no reason to stay around."

"If that doesn't take the cake," said Shirley, returning to the basement to sit with Signe and Aunt Wilma, who were still drinking coffee. "Now she's loading up all the flowers and not leaving a single bouquet for the altar."

"I can't help thinking that Einar would be very disappointed in his grandniece's behavior," said Aunt Wilma. "She hasn't been a bit friendly or cordial to anyone."

Signe agreed. "They were certainly not cut from the same cloth."

"Maybe that's it," said Shirley slowly. "Maybe that woman is not Einar's grandniece at all."

Signe and Aunt Wilma stared at her blankly.

"Let's look at the facts," she continued. "Maybe the phone number you called, Signe, was not Eleanore's any more. And when that woman heard about Einar's death and realized that you had seen the sole heir only once, she thought there might be some quick money to be made on the estate, so she took off in her pick-up to grab the loot."

"And she has a very pointed chin," added Signe. "I distinctly remember how square it was in Einar's picture. Of course, she hasn't smiled either, but we could maybe excuse that at a funeral."

"Now, Aunt Wilma," said Shirley, "you noticed the flashy purple ring. If that were Eleanore's birthstone ring, it should have been a garnet, since her birthday is probably in January, about the time Einar wrote her a check."

I wonder why she never cashed it," said Signe.

"Perhaps she never received it," said Shirley thoughtfully. "I think we should contact the sheriff on this one."

A few days later, Sheriff Roy Larson came to the Holmquist's where Aunt Wilma was enjoying afternoon coffee.

"I did some checking," he said, "and tracked down Einar's grandniece. She moved eight weeks ago and had never gotten Einar's check. She had given him her new address and phone number, but he must not have bothered to change the old numbers in his book."

"I'll have to hand it to you, Shirley. You did a good job on this one," conceded Ed.

"But there is still a loose end to tie up," said Shirley. "Why didn't that impostor cash Eleanore's birthday check? She'd certainly feel no guilt doing that when she tried to take Einar for everything she could."

"I'll bet if we talked to J.D. Folvaag at First State Bank, we'd discover she cashed the check on her way out of town," said Aunt Wilma.

Ed gulped down the last of his coffee and headed for the basement to paint the birdhouse he had just built.

Yup, it was that time of year.

CHAPTER 13

THE CASE OF

The Misplaced Lutheran Hymnal

The Misplaced Lutheran Hymnal

Shirley had a headache. She had just returned from the Altar Guild's annual inventory session at First Lutheran of the Good Shepherd where Miss Olive Thorson had made a royal fuss over a missing hymnal.

Three years ago Olive had given four green hymnals in memory of her parents, on the condition that they be placed in the racks of the pew in which the parents always sat. When the inventory showed one of the hymnals missing, she insisted that the Altar Guild members go through every hymnal in every pew rack to find it. And when that failed, she extended the search to every imaginable nook and cranny. By the time the committee had finished, there was no time to get anything else done.

Shirley and the other women were furious, but no one dared say anything or act as though the missing hymnal weren't important because Olive would take it as a rejection of her or her deceased parents.

Then, just as Shirley got home, Aunt Wilma called to ask if she would drive her to the hospital to see Elvina Skarsdahl who had fallen the previous night and broken her hip. And just as Shirley reached for the aspirin bottle, Ed burst through the door with the news that the bigwigs on the Heartsberg City Council had decided the library wasn't big enough, and they wanted to build a new one.

"Our taxes will go through the roof!" he said. "It doesn"t make sense either. They have so many books down there a guy couldn't read them all in a lifetime, and some of the junk written nowadays isn't worth reading even if there is time. Besides, anyone who reads all the time seems to lose his common sense."

Shirley didn't have time to discuss the library issue with Ed since she was due at Aunt Wilma's. "When it rains, it pours," she muttered, as she went out the door.

Shirley was relieved when Aunt Wilma didn't want to stay long at the hospital. Elvina was heavily medicated and talking nonsense. When she asked Aunt Wilma if she would report back to her on the Communists who were moving into the old boarded-up chicken hatchery in Heartsberg, Aunt Wilma told her she had better get some more rest. But Elvina was insistent. "You've got some time, Wilma. Go to the sheriff and tell him the Communists have started stockpiling weapons, and we could be in big trouble." Aunt Wilma, at a loss for words, told Elvina the nurse was coming, so she had to leave.

"I hope I never get like that," Aunt Wilma said to Shirley as they left the hospital parking lot.

"Oh, don't worry," Shirley laughed. "They say heavy medication brings out a person's subconscious. But you've lived a clean life, so you have nothing to be concerned about. All the talk about war and Communists come from Elvina's being too involved in the VFW Auxiliary."

When Shirley got home, Ed had a job lined up for

her. "Mrs. Lavonne Berquist came over and said the family was going to a Rodeo & Round-up Jamboree in Montana for a week. She wondered if you would water her plants and check the furnace while they are gone. She had this skeleton key right in her hand, so I had no choice but to tell her I supposed you would do it."

Shirley had always wanted to get a look inside that house. Lavonne had grown up there, but she and her husband Jim and their four kids had moved into the house only four months ago, right after Lavonne's mother, Agnes, had passed on.

Shirley had never known Agnes very well because she kept pretty much to herself. She attended services every Sunday but never joined Altar Guild, Circle, or any other organization. When Agnes' husband Leroy died, people from the church brought over food, but they were met on the front porch, thanked, and sent on their way. Shirley knew the pastor had gotten inside the house, but he was the only one.

Lavonne was five years older than Gloria Jean and had hung around a wild bunch of kids in high school. She had married a local Berquist boy, and they had opened Berquist's Boots, Buckle, & Bait Shop shortly thereafter. Shirley thought it a little disrespectful for Lavonne and Jim to move into her mother's home so soon after Agnes' death, but as Aunt Wilma had said, "Who's to say?"

"My, they must be spending every penny Agnes left them, taking four kids to a rodeo in Montana," said Shirley. "The furthest Agnes ever got was to Fargo to see her sister. I remember she would take the Red River

Special and visit for a week every summer. Honestly, young people today think money grows on trees. They think nothing of taking off on a pleasure trip."

The next morning when Shirley told Ed she was going to the Berquist house to check on things, Ed said, "You don't have to go yet. They just left an hour ago."

"Well," Shirley said, "Lavonne was probably so busy packing, she forgot to turn off a light or something. And those kids might have left the radio on. I'd hate if anything went wrong when I'm responsible."

I'll start upstairs, thought Shirley, as she turned the key in the lock.

The pillows weren't fluffed, she noticed, but things were picked up. As she opened the top drawer of the nightstand, she saw a King James Bible. Must have belonged to Agnes, she thought. She opened it to the page where a bookmark was placed. Now, why would she be reading Zechariah right before she died, Shirley wondered, as she closed the Bible and put it back in the drawer.

In the medicine cabinet, Shirley spotted some teeth. "Good grief, could Lavonne be that money hungry that she'd save her mom's teeth to melt down?" she said aloud. She remembered Agnes had looked a little hollow in the face when she was lying in the casket.

She headed down the basement. The furnace looked all right, but Shirley was amazed to see all the jars of dill and beet pickles. She wondered how Agnes had ever planned to eat them when she never had company.

In the living room, Shirley felt the plants to see if they needed water. They were moist, but she knew Lavonne hadn't bothered to fertilize them because they looked so spindly. She needs to put some egg shells on these if she ever expects them to amount to anything, she thought.

With popcorn under the couch pillows, Shirley knew Lavonne let her kids have run of the house. But Gloria Jean was no better, she reminded herself. She let Mary Jane eat wherever and whenever she pleased.

Lavonne's Confirmation Bible lay on an end table collecting dust. Shirley opened it and saw the purple and white crocheted cross the Altar Guild had given her when she was confirmed. It was badly yellowed, and Shirley knew Lavonne hadn't ever bothered to wash or starch it. They don't take care of things the way they used to, she thought, as she closed the Bible and walked toward the piano.

When she opened the piano bench, Shirley got the surprise of her life. There, on top of the *"Blue Moon"* sheet music was a green hymnal.

"Well, I'll be!" Shirley exclaimed as she opened it. It read "Given in memory of Mr. & Mrs. Adolph Thorson by Miss Olive Thorson."

When Shirley told Ed about the green hymnal, he was less than sympathetic. "I can't understand why you thought you had any business looking into their piano bench. Lavonne asked you to water her plants and check the furnace. She didn't ask you to go through her house with a fine tooth comb."

Shirley decided not to say any more. Ed just got upset if he thought she was meddling, so she called Aunt Wilma.

"Why would Lavonne have had a green hymnal in the first place?" she asked.

Aunt Wilma thought a minute. "I imagine she borrowed it to pick out some hymns for her mother's funeral and forgot to bring it back."

"Funny, I didn't think of that, Aunt Wilma. But now I've got to figure out how to get the hymnal out of there without Lavonne's knowing. Just remembering how upset Olive Thorson is, I can't in good conscience leave her hymnal in Lavonne's piano bench. On the other hand, it wouldn't be very Christian of me just to take it from Lavonne's house either. That would be a type of stealing, I think."

"Oh, I can help you with that, Shirley. I've got a green hymnal you can have. You know our church uses the black ones, but I had bought a green one just to see how liberal things had gotten. You take it, put it in Lavonne's piano bench, bring Olive's hymnal back to church, and if you don't say anything about it, no one will know the difference.

"And I've been thinking about something else, Shirley. Do you suppose Elvina knows something about Communists moving to Heartsberg? Maybe she wasn't way out in left field after all. If there were Communists on the committee that put the green hymnal together, who's to say they wouldn't move to Heartsberg?"

Shirley, obviously relieved that Aunt Wilma had solved the hymnal dilemma for her, said, "We'll work on that one, Aunt Wilma. You never know nowadays; you just never know."

CHAPTER 14

THE CASE OF

The Communist Plot to Conquer Heartsberg

The Communist Plot to Conquer Heartsberg

"Get a grip on yourself, Aunt Wilma, and I'll be right over," said Shirley, hanging up the phone.

Thank goodness Ed isn't home to hear about this phone call, she thought. I'd have a hard time explaining Aunt Wilma's theory that Russians are moving into Heartsberg.

My, she is really upset, thought Shirley, as she waited for Aunt Wilma to unbolt the lock on her front door.

"Now, sit down and start over," said Shirley. "You were so breathless on the phone that for a minute I thought it was going to be your time. But you look healthy enough now, so just relax, and I'll pour some coffee."

"When I think about what happened this morning," said Aunt Wilma, "I wish it were my time. I was out for my morning walk, and I happened to go by the old boarded-up chicken hatchery. Then I remembered Elvina Skarsdahl's crazy words in the hospital, and I thought I'd look around to put my mind at ease and prove her wrong.

"You'll never believe what I saw, Shirley. Behind the building was a pile of crates, big enough to hold the weapons Elvina talked about. And on the crates were foreign words. I looked around to make sure no one was watching me, and then I left as fast as I could. Then I heard footsteps, and I could imagine Communists tailing me and shooting me with the ammunition they had stockpiled because I had discovered their whereabouts.

"We have to do something, Shirley. I've read about Communists. When they get a good grip on a town, they shut down the churches and make everyone stand in line for food. Those over sixty even get mysterious diseases. No wonder people would rather be dead than red."

"You can't be worrying about anything as far-fetched as that, Aunt Wilma," said Shirley, reassuringly. "But I'll tell you what, let's go to the hatchery together tomorrow and do some investigating."

"I'm not so sure I want to put myself in danger again," said Aunt Wilma. "Besides, the crates are half covered with snow."

"That's no problem," said Shirley. "I'll bring along a whisk broom to brush off the snow, and you bring a pen and notebook so you can write down the foreign words as I read them to you."

TO BE CONTINUED

Reorder Form for *Shirley Holmquist & Aunt Wilma, Whodunit?*

Name ____________________

Address ____________________

City ____________ State ________ Zip ________

No. of Copies ______ @ $7.95/copy Subtotal ________

Postage & Handling $1.00 (per book) ________

MN Residents add 6% Sales Tax ________

Total ________

Send cash, check, or money order to Martin House Publications, Box 274, Hastings, MN 55033.

If you have not read my other books, *Cream and Bread* or *Second Helpings of Cream and Bread,* you must! You can order them from Martin House Publicatons for the price of $6.95 plus $1.00 each for shipping and handling.

For my free newsletter *THE MARTIN HOUSE HERALD,* send a self-addressed, stamped envelope to the address above.

Reorder Form for *Shirley Holmquist & Aunt Wilma, Whodunit?*

Name ____________________

Address ____________________

City ____________ State ________ Zip ________

No. of Copies ______ @ $7.95/copy Subtotal ________

Postage & Handling $1.00 (per book) ________

MN Residents add 6% Sales Tax ________

Total ________

Send cash, check, or money order to Martin House Publications, Box 274, Hastings, MN 55033.

If you have not read my other books, *Cream and Bread* or *Second Helpings of Cream and Bread,* you must! You can order them from Martin House Publicatons for the price of $6.95 plus $1.00 each for shipping and handling.

For my free newsletter *THE MARTIN HOUSE HERALD,* send a self-addressed, stamped envelope to the address above.

Reorder Form for *Shirley Holmquist & Aunt Wilma, Whodunit?*

Name ______________________________

Address ______________________________

City ______________ State ________ Zip ________

No. of Copies ______ @ $7.95/copy Subtotal ________

Postage & Handling $1.00 (per book) ________

MN Residents add 6% Sales Tax ________

Total ________

Send cash, check, or money order to Martin House Publications, Box 274, Hastings, MN 55033.

If you have not read my other books, *Cream and Bread* or *Second Helpings of Cream and Bread,* you must! You can order them from Martin House Publicatons for the price of $6.95 plus $1.00 each for shipping and handling.

For my free newsletter *THE MARTIN HOUSE HERALD,* send a self-addressed, stamped envelope to the address above.

Reorder Form for *Shirley Holmquist & Aunt Wilma, Whodunit?*

Name ______________________________

Address ______________________________

City ______________ State ________ Zip ________

No. of Copies ______ @ $7.95/copy Subtotal ________

Postage & Handling $1.00 (per book) ________

MN Residents add 6% Sales Tax ________

Total ________

Send cash, check, or money order to Martin House Publications, Box 274, Hastings, MN 55033.

If you have not read my other books, *Cream and Bread* or *Second Helpings of Cream and Bread,* you must! You can order them from Martin House Publicatons for the price of $6.95 plus $1.00 each for shipping and handling.

For my free newsletter *THE MARTIN HOUSE HERALD,* send a self-addressed, stamped envelope to the address above.

ABOUT THE AUTHOR

Janet Letnes Martin, daughter of the late John and Helen Klemetson Letnes, grew up in the rural setting of Hillsboro, North Dakota. Both her maternal and paternal grandparents came from Norway and helped settle this area. She received her B.A. from Augsburg College, Minneapolis, Minnesota, and furthered her studies at the University of Minnesota. In 1983 Janet wrote a family history book entitled *Reiste Til Amerika.* In 1984 and 1986, respectively, she co-authored *Cream and Bread* and *Second Helpings of Cream and Bread* with Allen Todnem of Hastings, Minnesota. She and her husband, Neil Martin of Newfolden, Minnesota, reside in Hastings, Minnesota, with their three daughters, Jennifer, Sarah, and Katrina.